THE
COUNTERFEIT
BRIDE

Other books by Nancy J. Parra:

The Morgan Family Historical Romance Series
Saving Samantha
A Wanted Man
Loving Lana
Wyoming Wedding
The Marryin' Kind
The Bettin' Kind
The Lovin' Kind

THE
COUNTERFEIT
BRIDE

•

Nancy J. Parra

AVALON BOOKS
NEW YORK

For my dear friend and mentor, Carolyn Brown.
Thank you for your stories and your friendship.

Published by Avalon Books,
an imprint of Thomas Bouregy & Co., Inc.
160 Madison Avenue, New York, NY 10016

Library of Congress Cataloging-in-Publication Data

Parra, Nancy J.
   The counterfeit bride / Nancy J. Parra.
      p. cm.
   ISBN 978-0-8034-7662-2
   1. Colorado—Fiction.   I. Title.
   PS3616.A765C68 2011
   813'.6—dc22
                                    2010046219

PRINTED IN THE UNITED STATES OF AMERICA
ON ACID-FREE PAPER
BY RR DONNELLEY, BLOOMSBURG, PENNSYLVANIA

Chapter One

Colorado, 1877

Marrying Donovan West was the best idea Lillian Picken had ever had, and she'd had a lot of good ideas.

Lillian looked out the glass window of her room above her general store. Mountains surrounded her, sleeping giants of purple and pine. Lovely. Lillian allowed a secret smile. She was exactly where she'd always dreamed she'd be, all thanks to Donovan. It was the perfect life, except for one little truth she hoped no one ever discovered.

Donovan West did not exist.

Lillian had made him up.

She dismissed any guilt about the lie. After all, she had tried to do things properly and had been turned away at every point. It seemed the modern male did not believe the female mind capable of handling the complexities of running a business. But growing up an orphan had taught Lillian grit and determination and a great deal about human nature.

It was a true fact that people believed what they wanted. That was how she was able to tell such a lovely and profitable lie.

Not that it was a big lie. She had merely introduced herself as Mrs. Donovan West and said that her husband had a dream of opening a general store. When the one in Silverton came up for sale, her "husband" sent her to buy it, hoping that soon he would come to join her. When the banker had asked if Donovan was in the army, she merely had nodded. From there it was easy. Everyone assumed he was busy keeping the frontier safe but would be home as soon as his commission had ended, which Lillian knew would be a very, very long time from now.

1

So she was free to open her store. Free to enjoy the life she built with scrimped earnings, a keen wit, and a wily imagination.

She buttoned the cuffs of her new work dress and noted the pinkened sky. Soon the sun would be up, and the miners would be on their way to the mountain. The silver rush had brought a stampede of men into Silverton, along with their families. The town had tripled in size, and sales were booming. In fact, she made it a habit of checking in with the other local businesses every Wednesday morning to take their weekly orders. It was a good way to build sales and remain on friendly terms with anyone who might consider becoming a competitor.

Lillian stepped out her back door and into the alley that separated her store from the outbuildings behind it. Breathing in the morning mountain air, she felt as though she could take on the world.

"Mornin', Red."

Bart Johnson emerged from the shadows. Frowning, she ignored him and hurried down the alley toward Main Street.

Snaking his hand out, Bart grabbed her by the arm before she could escape. "I said, good morning, Red."

"My name is Mrs. West." Lillian yanked her arm out of his reach. She tried to move past him, but he blocked her way.

"Yeah, you keep tellin' everyone you're married, but I ain't never seen the guy." Bart's dark eyes gleamed in the early-morning light. A shiver ran down Lillian's back. Bart Johnson had a reputation for being ugly. It was a reputation she didn't want to know about firsthand.

"Of course you wouldn't see him. Donovan is off defending this country."

"Too bad he's not here to defend you. The way I see it, a man who don't defend his own ain't a real man." Bart reached out and picked up the loose end of her bonnet ribbon. Disgusted, Lillian stepped away. The action untied her ribbon.

"You would prefer the country was left defenseless?" She clamped her hand on her hat to keep it from falling off.

"Only defense I need is right here." He patted the gun

holster on his hip. "I take care of my own." His gaze bored into hers.

"Well, so does Donovan." Lillian pushed past him. "Good day!"

Her heart pounded in her chest. Freedom was two steps away. She knew that Mr. Huckabee would be opening the barbershop about now. There was no way Bart would cause a scene where decent folks could see.

"A real man wouldn't let a woman like you walk around alone." He took a quick step forward and managed to catch the hem of her dress under his boot, stopping her cold. "It ain't safe." Bart stepped in close behind her and ran his hand along her arm. "A real man would have a little treasure like you tucked away in his bed, not paradin' around town teasing all the rest of us."

Lillian froze to the spot. She had gone from fear to downright anger the moment he touched her. "Get your hands off me!"

"Or what?" His rank breath dampened her ear. "Your man gonna come git me?"

Lillian's control snapped. She fisted her hand around the ivory handle of her parasol and jammed it hard into Bart's gut. He let out an odd *woof* sound, doubled over, and hit the dirt. "You keep your hands off me, or *I'll* come get you." Lillian's heart raced. Her hands trembled as she picked up the bonnet that had fallen off in the scuffle. Then with as much dignity as she could muster, she brushed the dust off her skirt and stepped out into the street.

A glance at the town clock as she retied the ribbon on her hat told her that if she didn't hurry she would be late for her Wednesday business rounds. Silverton was small. Even a few minutes late would cause people to ask questions, and she had a reputation to maintain. She hurried across the street to meet Millie Baker at the hat shop before the clock struck eight.

He'd watched the encounter from the other end of the alley. In fact, he'd been a second away from exposing his whereabouts when the furious redhead had taken the suspect down. Interest and pride filled him at the sight.

He'd never seen the like in his life. Oh, he'd known some feisty women. His mother and sister qualified as being able to handle themselves, but he'd never seen a gorgeous redhead take a man down with a parasol. The idea appealed to him. A woman like that would defend her family to the death. Something his frail wife had been unable to do.

With Susan, he'd taken one look at her porcelain beauty and fallen instantly in love—the kind of love a man should never marry. All he'd wanted to do was put her on a shelf and keep her safe forever.

Forever hadn't happened. Susan had died in childbirth, taking the baby with her. He hadn't wanted another woman since. For him, love had led to death. He refused to let his heart murder another. No matter how many times his mother and sister had knocked him upside the head and told him he was wrong. He hadn't even felt the rush of desire in two years.

That is until today, when he'd nearly stepped out of the shadows to rescue a petite redhead. The same redhead with flashing blue eyes that had neatly handled a man a full head taller and twice her size.

Somewhere inside him a dam burst, and he felt more alive than he had in years. Too bad he was on a case. Still, it couldn't hurt to find out everything he could about her. What had she said to Johnson? Ah, yes, her name was Mrs. West. Well, now that was a place to start.

"Heard talk Parssal's mine is bringing in more than he can handle." Will Stewart leaned against the counter. "They're sayin' he's lookin' to hire extra workers."

"Is that right?" Lillian asked absently. Will was there for his weekly stock up on supplies. Lillian knew he liked to talk. It really didn't matter if she answered. Still, she figured it was good form to keep the conversation going. The longer he stayed in the store, the more likely he was to buy more than what was on the list he had given her. "Are you thinking of giving up on your own mine and going to work for him?"

"Naw, I ain't the kind to work for another."

"I know most people feel that way." She marked off the goods on his list. "Say, I've got a barrel of pickles due in next week. How many do you want me to save for you?"

"Dill pickles or sweets?"

"Dill this time."

"Put your finger in them, and they'll be sweet," he said.

Surprised, Lillian looked up from the list in time to catch his slow wink. "I'm a married woman, Will."

"Ain't no harm in flirtin'." Will's beard-roughened cheeks went pink. "I have to keep my practice up. You never know when some pretty young widow will arrive in town."

"I didn't know you were in a courtin' mood, Will."

"I might be." Will shoved his hands into the pockets of his cotton pants. "Nothing wrong with that neither. Got my cabin all built, and the mine is keeping me in money. I figure I got a lot to offer a nice lady too." He turned his chocolate brown puppy-dog eyes on her. "But it's been a while since I've been around 'em, you know? So's I thought I'd practice every chance I got."

"Did you take a bath?" Lillian studied him thoughtfully. Will was in his early thirties, and with most of the dust off him, he wasn't half bad looking.

"This mornin'." He shrugged. "Paid a good dollar for a nice hot one and some of that fancy soap over at Kelly's."

"Slicked your hair back too." Lillian took in his dark hair plastered against his head. "Could use a new hat though."

"You think?" Will eyed his dusty hat critically. "This one works good. Got it all broke in."

"Let me see it." Lillian took his hat and looked it over. "Yes, I see what you mean. This is good felt and formed just right to keep the rain off the back of your neck."

"See—"

"But . . ."

"What?"

"Well, this hat is good. Useful. Still . . ." She bit her lip and didn't take her gaze off her customer's hat. With any luck she was going to make a sale. A good sale and possibly help Will find his match. At least that's what she told herself.

"Still, what?"

"A lady, especially a pretty widow, is going to be looking for a man of some means."

"I told you, I got means. I got the mine and a nice cabin with a bedroom and a loft."

"I bet it's right pretty too," Lillian said. "But this hat, this hat says you're still working on your means. Now don't get me wrong. It's a good hat for working and when the weather is bad. But if I were a widow and looking for a man of means . . ."

"You'd what?"

"Well, now, it's silly because I'm not a widow." She handed him back his hat. "Don't mind my musing."

"Hold on, now," he said. "If you were a widow, what?"

"If I were a widow and I were looking for a man of means to support me, well, I'd sure be impressed by a man who could afford two hats. You know, one for working and one for, well, courting and church on Sunday and such." She shrugged. "But that's me."

"A man with two hats."

"That's only me." She looked down at the list he had given her and carefully checked off the items she had already wrapped for him.

"You got hats, right?"

"Oh, yes, we sell all kinds of hats for men."

He wandered over to the corner and looked at the hats on the shelf. "Which of these hats would you consider Sunday-go-to-meetin' hats?"

She put down the list and schooled her features. "Well, now, like I said, it was simply my opinion and that doesn't matter since I'm not a widow."

"Which hat looks like a man of means to you?" He picked up a hat. It was one of her cheaper felt hats.

"That one's nice." She quickly took it from him. "But this one says you're a rich man." She pulled down the beaver hat she'd bought on a whim and hadn't been able to sell. She brushed the dust off on the side of her sleeve and stretched up to place it on his head.

Will dipped his head low enough for her to put the hat on him and straightened. To her relief, the hat actually fit. The catalog had one thing right. This hat was made for a dandy. Will frowned. "Well, what do you think?"

"Hmmm," she said as she studied him from all sides. "It sure is pretty."

"Pretty like a lady's hat?" His voice cracked and he reached up quick to take off the hat.

She placed her hand on his arm to stop him. "Pretty as in the beaver coat looks shiny and . . . well . . . rich." She nodded. "Yes, I'd say you look like a very rich man, Will Stewart."

"Rich, huh?"

"Well, it is a four-dollar hat." She bit her lip. "But we're friends, and it looks so good on you. I'll sell it to you for a dollar and fifty cents."

"A whole dollar and a half?" Will frowned.

Lillian pulled out a hand mirror. "I'm telling you, this will have all the ladies in two counties noticing you. See?" She handed him the mirror as the bell on the door jangled.

"Lillian." Joyce Huckabee hurried inside. "My goodness." She stopped and put her hand to her chest as if to catch her breath. "I came all this way to scold you and here I am out of breath."

"Scold me?" Lillian moved around the display of canned peaches. "Whatever for?"

"For keeping that beautiful man to yourself."

"Excuse me?"

"She's selling me this hat." Will's cheeks grew red again. "Not keeping me to herself. She's married."

"I wasn't talking about you." Joyce glanced Will's way and looked at Lillian and then back at Will. "Is that a new hat?"

"Yeah," Will said. "What do you think?"

"Well, it certainly makes you look . . ."

"Manly? Wealthy?"

"Different." Joyce stepped toward him. "Is that made of beaver?"

Lillian nodded. Joyce was fifteen years older than Lillian and enjoyed being a woman in the know when it came to things going on around town. Her husband ran the barbershop and any bit of gossip went swiftly from ear to ear.

"Excuse me, Joyce, what were you talking about?"

"This beaver hat is lovely. Can I get one for Ed?"

"It's the only one I have," Lillian said.

"And she sold it to me . . . for two dollars." Will reached into his pocket and pulled out two bills.

Lillian took his money before he could change his mind. "I'll get a nice box to keep it from crushing."

"Don't bother. I'm going to wear it out," he said. "I heard that Widow Sheridan was meeting with her sister at the tearoom this afternoon."

"Then here, let me cut off the price tag." Lillian pulled a short pair of shears out of her apron pocket, snipped the tag off the hat, and handed it back to him. "You go on," she said. "Tea time's near over."

"Thank you, Lillian." Will smiled. "I'll be back for the rest in about an hour."

"Take your time." Lillian waved as he hurried out the door.

"Will lookin' for a wife?" Joyce eyed him through the glass as he hurried across the street.

Lillian smoothed the two dollar bills and went back around the counter to put them in her lockbox. "He's thinking about it."

"I'll warn the ladies." Joyce came over to the counter. "Honey, I had no idea your man was so handsome." She put her hand on her chest again. "I swear, when he introduced himself I nearly fell out of my chair."

"I'm sorry? I don't . . ."

"Your Donovan," Joyce said. "He came into the barbershop this afternoon for a trim. He had everyone abuzz. Seems he is quite the war hero."

"My Donovan?" Lillian repeated.

"Your husband, silly." Joyce playfully slapped Lillian's arm. "Here we were all thinking he'd actually abandoned you, what with him taking so long to give up his commission and come home."

"My husband went into the barbershop today?" It was preposterous, of course. Donovan West did not exist. There was no way he could get a haircut. "My husband, Donovan West?"

"Yes, silly, your husband. What other Donovan West would there be?"

A chill ran down Lillian's spine and pooled funny in her stomach. "There wouldn't be another Donovan West," she said, fervently as if a prayer. Which it was. There was no way on God's green earth there was a real Donovan West, was there?

"Of course not," Joyce said. "You look a little pale. Are you all right?"

"I'm fine. I think I'm going to sit down a moment." Lillian found the stool behind the counter. "When exactly did Donovan come into the barbershop? I mean, his last letter told me he had orders to head south and stop an uprising."

"Oh, honey, he came in after dinner. Said he had a pocket full of silver and thought he'd get cleaned up a bit before he surprised . . ." Joyce paused, her eyes widening. "Oh my, I went and spoiled his surprise now, didn't I?"

"Oh, I don't think so," Lillian said. "I'm pretty much surprised. Is he still at the barbershop?"

"Last I knew."

"Would you watch the store for me a moment?" Lillian shot up off the stool. If there was one thing being an orphan had taught her, it was that adversity was something to be met head on. She refused to hole up in her shop and wring her hands in worry. No sirree, she was going to face this man and call his bluff outright.

Lillian didn't give Joyce a chance to answer as she raced out. The barbershop was next door, and she needed to keep going before she changed her mind. After all, this had to be a bad joke, right? It wasn't April Fool's Day, but Joyce could tell some tales.

She stormed down the boardwalk and into the barbershop, and then stopped short. Four men looked up from what they were doing and stared. The barbershop wasn't a place for women, at least not usually.

She looked at each man. Which one was the man claiming to be her husband? She dismissed the two playing checkers right off. Tom and John Peckich were brothers and came in every Monday while their ma did laundry. Mr. Huckabee stood behind the barber chair. That left only one man. A tall and lanky gentleman with hair the color of aspen leaves in the fall. He watched her with an unsettling intensity in his deep-green eyes. She swallowed the tiniest fracture of fear when his gaze ran over her.

"Hello." He smiled a bit too knowingly.

"Lillian, what brings you to the barbershop?" Mr. Huckabee asked with a twinkle in his kind eyes.

"Joyce told me my husband was here," Lillian said firmly. Or at least she thought it was firm, but it might have come out more like a whisper. Her heart pounded so loudly she wasn't sure of anything. She couldn't take her eyes off the lanky man who had settled into the barber chair.

"You just missed him." Mr. Huckabee lathered soap in his shaving mug and applied it to the man's face.

"I missed him?" Lillian's mouth was dry. So the handsome stranger wasn't claiming to be her husband. She didn't know whether to be relieved or disappointed.

"He said something about stopping by the feed store."

"The feed store?" she echoed, feeling a tad bit foolish. The man in the barber chair winked at her, and it startled her enough to make her stop staring. What was wrong with everybody today? She swallowed hard and concentrated on the barber's bald pate. "He was heading to the feed store?"

"That's what he said."

"Why?"

"Guess you'll have to ask him." The barber sharpened his

razor on the strop that hung on the side of the chair. "Sure was nice to finally meet him though."

"Are you sure you weren't mistaken?" When the men looked at her funny, she stumbled on. "I mean, my husband is supposed to be south of Colorado Springs. I thought I'd be the first to know if he weren't."

"Hmm," Mr. Huckabee said. "Now, he did say something about his arrival being a surprise and all." He finished shaving the man and pulled a hot towel out of the container that sat on top of the potbelly stove. Then he gingerly placed it on the stranger's face. "Seems like my Joyce jumped the gun a bit on that one. Sorry to spoil it for you. Don't worry, though, I'm sure he's headed to the store right now to see you."

"Don't worry," she couldn't stop herself from muttering. There was a man running around town impersonating her husband, and she wasn't to worry about it? Right. "Good day, gentlemen."

She left the barbershop not knowing what to do. It would be easy to spend the rest of the day chasing down a man calling himself her husband. She'd make a fool of herself all right if she did that. Why, the whole time he could be standing right beside her, and she wouldn't even know it.

A glance across the street told her that everyone at the tearoom had noted her progress in and out of the barbershop. She forced herself to smile and wave. The ladies looked away quickly.

Lillian shook her head, angry at herself for running willy-nilly into the male sanctuary and giving the town something to talk about. She frowned and crossed her arms over her chest. Seemed like the best course of action now was to do nothing.

After all, this was probably one big bad joke. Mr. and Mrs. Huckabee could really pull a good one if they wanted to. The thing to do was go back to work and pretend nothing had happened.

Stewing, she uncrossed her arms and headed down the boardwalk. It wasn't all that far to go, down the boardwalk, across the alley, and then back up to the boardwalk that ran in front of the store, but she felt eyes on her every step of the way. Seems whoever claimed to be her husband had caused a big stir. Well, she would correct that right away. Let him come into the store—her store—and try to take over. Why, she'd—

"Darling!"

With her mind on other things, Lillian ran smack dab into a warm wall. Strong hands held her by the shoulders, stopping her from bouncing backward. She looked up into the deepest, bluest eyes she had ever seen and a shiver of something close to lightning ran from the top of her head to the bottom of her toes.

She blinked and opened her mouth to excuse herself. The man with the deep blue eyes took that moment to pull her into his chest, bend down, and kiss her full on the lips. Shock followed the lightning in her system as she was assailed by the smell of bay rum warmed by male skin, the feel of strong muscle under her palms.

In that instant, her thoughts froze like a rabbit spotting a fox.

It was the only way she could explain what happened next. Instead of pushing him off and slapping his face, she closed her eyes. For one moment she savored the unexpected and overwhelming sensuality and security of a man's arms.

Chapter Two

He shouldn't have kissed her.

Really, he shouldn't have, but he couldn't help it. He'd wanted to kiss her ever since he'd seen her take down Bart Johnson. Now he had the perfect opportunity. This was his time to take his place as her husband, and a husband was free to kiss his wife in public. Not the way he wanted to kiss her, but enough to give credence to his identity.

What he hadn't expected was her response. Instead of shoving him off, she melted against him. Dang. It took every ounce of his self-discipline to keep the kiss decent. He broke contact and quickly tucked her hand under his arm to keep her from slapping him. He shouldn't have worried. One look at her face had his pride swelling. She looked all dewy-eyed and amazed.

"Surprise," he said. "I've decided I miss you."

"What?" She looked up at him, and he knew that he had only a few more seconds before she'd be kicking him in the shin.

"Darling, let's go inside the shop. There are far too many eyes and ears on the street." Donovan hustled her into the shop and to the back room. The eyes of the town were on them until he pulled the calico curtain that separated the back from the front of the store.

He let her go and moved a safe distance away. "Hello, darling, I'm home."

"I don't understand." She stared at him, stunned.

He could see her mind working out her current situation, and it was all he could do not to grin at her. But he had to remain serious. He had only a few minutes to figure out how far she'd let him go with this ruse.

"What's not to understand, love?" He leaned against the wall. "I'm home from the war and ready to take my rightful place at the store."

"Your rightful place?" She frowned. "Wait!" She held up her hand and narrowed her eyes. "Before this goes any further, who the sugar are you?"

"I'm your husband, darling," he said. "Have I been away so long that you don't recognize me?"

"You, sir, are not my husband."

He watched her struggle with what to do with him.

"Yes, I am." Donovan took a step toward her. Maybe if he kissed her again . . .

"Don't come anywhere near me." Lillian backed up into the corner with one hand out in front of her, as if to ward him off, and the other behind her back. When she grabbed the broom in the corner, he stopped short and held up his hands.

"Darling," he crooned. "Put that broom down. You know I'd never hurt you."

"No, I don't." She narrowed her eyes. "I don't know you."

"You kissed me. Are you telling me that you are in the habit of kissing strange men on the street?"

She gasped and swung the broom at him. "I do nothing of the sort!"

He grinned and ducked. That got her. She had to admit that either she was a loose woman or he was her husband. He grabbed the broom and hauled her up against his chest.

She was small but curvy in all the right places. Her auburn hair smelled of violets, and it frightened him how well she fit up under his heart. Still, instead of letting her go, he pulled her closer.

"Of course, you wouldn't run around kissing strange men on a public street, darling," he said, low next to her ear. It was a tempting little ear, pale and shell-shaped. He stopped himself from nibbling. It was a little too soon for that. Darn it. "Everyone knows the only man you'd kiss is your husband."

"That's right." Pride showed in her beautiful eyes.

He grinned. "Gotcha, sweetheart."

Her eyes grew wide, and she pushed at him. "Let me go!"

"Only after you admit the truth."

"What truth?"

"You kissed me."

"So, what if I did?"

"That can mean only one thing."

"That you ambushed me?"

"No, silly, that I'm your husband, Donovan West." He held his hands out like a silly circus ringleader at the "tada" moment.

She opened and closed her mouth and then paused, her blue eyes revealing terrible thoughts. Good thing he was quick. He managed to move his foot before she could come down on his instep. He let her go to give her some time. In the thick silence, he pulled out an available chair, turned it around, and sat down.

"You can't be Donovan West," she argued vehemently, albeit quietly. They were both very much aware of the thinness of the curtain that separated them from the rest of the store and listening customers.

"Why not?"

"Because I—"

"You what?" He leaned his arms across the back of the chair. Sitting down, he had a good view of her curves, set off by the white apron tied around her tiny waist. "You what?"

"This is my store," she said, changing the subject. "I worked hard for this store."

"Our store," he said. "The deed is recorded to Mr. and Mrs. Donovan West. That would be you and me."

She shook her head. "No."

His heart went out to her for a moment. Bet when she made up her man she never thought someone could show up and claim to be him. Reality hurt. He would be gentle with her. "Come here." He held out his hand. "I promise I won't bite."

"What if I do?" she groused. He laughed and took her hand. It was small and delicate in his. She was something, his new "wife." He wasn't quite sure what he was going to do with her yet, but for now it seemed they called a truce.

"Well, then I'll be careful to avoid your teeth," he said softly, and she relaxed a little as his thumb stroked the back of her hand. Of course, the back of the chair put a small barrier between them. He'd go slow, let her get used to him, like a new colt getting used to its bridle. "What say we go out there and ease folks' curiosity?" He squeezed her hand. "From what I hear, everyone has been dying to meet me. What could it hurt to let them, now that I'm home to stay?"

She pulled her hand away from his and tucked them both behind her back as the doorbells jangled. "What say you go back to wherever you came from?" Her chin moved up in defiance. "People can think whatever they want. From my experience they do anyway."

The bells rang again as another customer entered the store. He could hear people gathering on the other side of the curtain. "We'll be out in a moment," he called over his shoulder. "After we settle some things."

She gasped. "There is nothing to settle," she said in a loud whisper.

"Oh, there's a lot to settle, darling." In one smooth motion he stood, pushed the chair back against the wall, and removed the space between them.

"Don't touch me," she warned.

"I wouldn't think of it." Then he did the hardest thing he'd done in a long, long time. Donovan turned his back on her and went out to greet the people crowding the store.

Lillian turned over the CLOSED sign and locked the door. It had been a busy and profitable evening. Who knew having a real man show up as her husband would be good for business?

She leaned against the door, her hand still on the knob behind her. "There is one thing I'd like to know."

"What's that?" He balanced his chair on two legs and stretched out his arms until he cradled his head in his hands.

"What is your name?"

"Donovan West."

He grinned at her as if she was a fool, but she knew she was not. They both knew he wasn't Donovan West. Yet, he had her firmly trapped. If she admitted she made him up, then he could go to the authorities and her contracts would be null and void. So what she had to do was somehow get him to admit that he was an imposter.

"You can call me Don if you like." He walked toward her. " 'Dear husband' would be better."

She hightailed it behind the counter. "Donovan will do, if that is what you insist."

"Oh, I insist." He followed her. She did her best to ignore him and pulled the cashbox out from its space.

He was difficult to ignore. First off, the man was simply too big for his own good. Why, he filled up her entire sense of the room. Second, he smelled wonderful, all warm and masculine. Third, he had rid the town of any doubts it might have harbored of her being anything other than a married woman.

It only made matters worse that she had sold a week's worth of goods in the process of their introductions.

She opened the cashbox and pretended to count the money. He leaned against the counter and watched her. It made her fingers tremble to know that those blue eyes were focused on her, even if it was merely to see how much money she counted.

"Stop it."

"Stop what?" He sounded a bit too innocent, and it annoyed her.

"Stop watching me," she said. "Don't you have anything better to do?"

"Better than watch my bride count our daily profits?"

"You mean my profits," she said. "And if you knew anything at all, you would know that nearly eighty percent of this money goes to pay the bills."

"We have bills?"

She slammed the box shut and looked him square in the

eye. Big mistake. He simply took her breath away. All thought drained right out of her brain. He was so big, so masculine, and so darn close. His thick black hair waved and, new haircut or not, fell over his forehead, making her want to push it aside.

It didn't help that her skin tingled just to look at him. Her lips itched to touch his again, just once, to see if it was merely the surprise of the last kiss that had her sinking.

He grinned at her. It was a crooked, knowing grin that was at once a dare and an "I told you so" at the same time. How on earth did he accomplish that in one look? It must be practiced.

She took a step back. It was better to put some space between them. He had spent the entire late afternoon and evening in her shop, taking up all the air, touching her in absent ways. She needed time to breathe, to think, to figure out how the heck everything had gone so very wrong.

"Good night." She picked up the cashbox and walked to the back of the shop. He didn't say anything in return. With any luck, she'd make it up the stairs before he understood where she was going. Thank goodness she had had the foresight to put a bolt on the apartment door.

She marched up the back stairs, tucking the cashbox under her arm. When she walked through the door, she closed it quickly behind her.

She was not quick enough. He stuck his foot in the crack. When she put her entire will into closing the door, it did not budge. He merely looked at her as if she were an insignificant thing. She sent him her most evil look. Instead of withering, he merely smiled.

"You are beautiful when you're angry."

"You, sir, are cruel." Giving up, she stormed across the apartment. It was growing dark, so by habit she went to the small table near the window, set the cashbox down, and lit the hurricane lamp.

"You've done wonders with the place." He moved around it, touching the lace she placed so carefully on the back of the small settee. It was clear that he was out of place in the small but comfortably feminine room. "I take it the bedroom is through here."

She practically ran to beat him to the door of the only other room. "Don't you dare!" She held her arms wide to block him from going into her personal space. As an orphan, it had taken her years to be able to afford a room that was all her own. She vowed she'd fight to the death to keep it that way.

"Dare what, sweetheart?" He peeked over her shoulder.

"A woman's bedroom is a sacred place," she stated firmly. "You, sir, have not been invited in."

He laughed. It was a deep, rumbling sound that comforted her when it should have irritated her. Why? She'd have to worry that one out later.

"Okay, love." He shoved his hands into his pockets. "You win this one." Donovan wandered away from the door and relief washed over her.

He might be a big oaf who accosted her on the street, but he was gentleman enough to leave the bedroom to her. *Darn it, why had I allowed him to kiss me?*

She watched him walk through the room and couldn't help but realize that she had gotten herself into this situation. If she hadn't kissed him back, the entire town would have come to her aid.

Instead, they assumed that he was her husband and rushed to welcome him. She was well and truly trapped. How could she explain her actions without sounding like a loose woman? Loose women were not fit for the company of others. The townswomen would cross the street if they saw her. No one would come near the store. If the town found out she was not married to this man, she'd have to close up shop and sneak out in the middle of the night.

He had been quite smart about it all and she, on the other hand, had been a dope.

But not for long. Surely he underestimated her. All men did. He wasn't going to get away with this charade. She'd think of something to stop him. All she had to do was figure out who he really was and why he thought he could get away with pretending to be her husband.

Donovan West was a good solid name. He liked the way it sounded on his tongue. He was glad there wasn't a real flesh-and-blood man who owned it.

It had taken him exactly two hours and a telegram to Denver to figure out what the heck she was up to. It seemed everyone liked the little scam artist so much they never really questioned why they had never seen her "husband."

Donovan had seen one too many cons, and his suspicious mind had not taken long to ferret out the truth. She was no more married than he was. She'd made it up. He had no idea where she had gotten her original stake, but she had come into town a year ago and carefully manipulated everyone into believing that her fake husband Donovan West was the true owner of the highly profitable general store.

Before he left, Donovan planned to ask her about the ruse. Find out why she had done it. After all, this was a modern age. Women were known to own establishments, such as boarding-houses and dress shops.

He'd watched her carefully and listened to the way she spoke to the people. She had a good rapport with them. Her sales pitches were easy and subtle, and yet, he suspected she could sell ice to an Eskimo if she wanted to.

He glanced at the door to her bedroom. Lillian had barri-caded herself inside about an hour ago, leaving him with one small lamp and the darn settee. He knew she had a handgun in her dresser drawer. In his line of work it was always best to do some snooping, and he'd taken all the ammunition. So, if she thought to use it, which she hadn't so far, he was safe. He stretched his long legs over the settee armrest and wondered if he wouldn't be better off on the floor.

Heck, he'd managed floors before when he was on a case. He thought about his partner, Kane McCormick, firmly and com-fortably ensconced in Mrs. Blake's boardinghouse. Now that was one pretty widow who didn't mind a man looking twice.

He eyed the door again. Mrs. Blake might be pretty, but she was nothing like Lillian West. He tucked his hands behind his head and closed his eyes. Ah, yes, Lillian. She was a smart little thing with gumption and flashing blue eyes that challenged a man.

He quit grinning when he thought of the kiss. It had been a brilliant move on his part—not that he'd planned it—when she'd run into him with a full head of steam. He had thought of nothing else but kissing her. It had been a long, long time since a single, simple kiss had affected him. Maybe because there had been an element of danger in it. After all, for all he knew she was fully capable of laying him low. He'd seen her do it to Bart Johnson.

But she hadn't done it to him.

He took a deep breath, ignoring the rapid beat of his heart. No sense in allowing himself to get all riled up until he knew for certain she wasn't a part of the counterfeit ring he and Kane had come out to bust up. That thought made him frown.

He hadn't figured she could be involved. It could be why she made up the whole marriage ruse. A general store would be the perfect place to launder money. He sat up straight. The general store was a good place to trade silver for cash. From what he'd seen today, a lot of money went through her hands. She kept a great deal of silver in the bargain.

He scowled, sat back, and pushed his hat down over his eyes. He knew she was a con artist, but was she also involved with a counterfeit ring? As members of the new Secret Service, Donovan and Kane had broken up their fair share of counterfeit rings. He'd never run into a member who looked and acted like Lillian West.

Something about her made him want to draw her against him and protect her from herself. How was he going to protect her if she were involved in this ring?

Lillian's stomach rumbled, and she sat up in bed. There was simply no sleeping, and it was entirely *his* fault. If he had not shown up, she would be safe and soundly asleep. Instead,

she was behind a locked door, too nervous to go out to her own
cupboard and find a late-night snack.

A snack she wouldn't even need if she had thought to eat
supper. But she hadn't done that either. He had thrown her off
her schedule, coming into her apartment and taking up all the
space, so that all she could think about was retreating to her
bedroom.

Lillian scowled at the moonlight that glowed through her tiny
bedroom window. She threw the covers off and got up. Moving
the lace curtain aside, she looked out.

Everything was closed at three in the morning. It would be
two hours before the café, which catered to miners, would
open for breakfast. She glanced at her door.

Her stomach growled again, and she put her hand on it. She
had spent her fair share of time hungry in this world. She'd be
darned if she let anything or anyone come between her and a
meal again.

Mind made up, Lillian pulled on her robe, belted it tightly
around her waist, and cautiously opened the door. It didn't make
a sound. She peered out through the crack between the door and
the jamb.

There he was, sprawled out on the settee. He looked horribly uncomfortable. Served him right. Her stomach grumbled
loudly, and she pressed it. The sound froze her to the spot.
Had he heard her?

He didn't move. His hat covered his eyes, and his legs dan-
gled awkwardly over the arm of the settee. She couldn't tell if
he was awake or asleep.

Lillian bit her lip and waited for him to give himself away.
He didn't, and her stomach threatened to protest louder.

In for a penny, in for a pound. She slid around the door and
into the main room of her apartment. Maybe if she were quiet
enough, she could be in and out without his even knowing it.

His position never changed, and she grew brave. It was only
a short distance to the cupboard, where she had a tin of biscuits
and some leftover apple pie. The thought of the pie had her
mouth watering. She glanced at the man. He didn't look very

dangerous right now. His boots were neatly placed by the foot of the settee, and his sock-covered feet had to be numb from the awkward position.

It was hard not to snicker. Okay, if she were of a good heart, she'd feel sorry for him. But she couldn't, not when he'd taken over her life without so much as a how-do-you-do.

Unless of course you counted the kiss. No, she wasn't going to think about that. Touching her lips to keep them from tingling in memory, she inched toward the cabinet, being careful to avoid the squeaky board that would give her away.

As quiet as a mouse, she pulled out a drawer and gathered a butter knife, a fork, and a napkin. She glanced over her shoulder to see his outlined form still on the settee as she closed the drawer. With great care, she opened the cupboard and gently picked up the pie plate.

"Apple pie is my favorite."

Startled, Lillian squealed, whipped around, and came face to chest with the man. His hands covered hers to keep her from dropping the pie. They were warm and large.

"Didn't mean to scare you."

Lillian looked up into the sharp shadowed features of his masculine face. "Yes, you did," she accused. "Why else would you sneak across the room?"

"I heard a noise," he explained. "When I saw a figure near the cupboard, I reacted. It's a habit I have."

"It's a bad habit." She realized that his thumbs caressed the back of her hands, sending tingles up her arms and into her chest. "Stop that!" She pulled back. She couldn't step away, as there was no space between her and the cupboard he had her up against.

"Stop what?" he asked innocently, stroking her hands.

"Standing so close," she said a bit breathlessly. "It isn't decent."

"Darling, anything a man and his wife do in the privacy of their home is decent."

"We are not man and wife."

"We've already had this conversation." He slid his hands up

her arms to cup her elbows and draw her impossibly closer. "Remember?"

He dipped his head, and she sucked in a breath anticipating his touch.

"I kissed you," he whispered so close his breath tickled her lips. His words smelled of mint and promise. "And you aren't the kind of woman who kisses strange men on the street."

"No, I'm not." She tried to focus her gaze on something decent. All she saw was his sensual mouth. Her hands clung to the pie pan, the scent of apple pie and cinnamon mixing with warm male skin.

Her own skin tingled. He was a breath away, all big and warm and so incredibly male. Had she ever been in a situation this intimate? Never. So how could she have known how she would react?

"Oh, dear." She breathed against his skin.

"What?" he asked gently.

"I think I'm going to kiss you," she replied. Before she could lean forward, he crushed her against him. His mouth found hers, and she swore she saw sparks fill the room as she closed her eyes.

Chapter Three

It was official. The man could make her toes curl. She never felt so excited, so alive as when his mouth was firm and pliant on hers. His skin smelled exotic, yet familiar. His mouth was warm and smooth in comparison to the roughness of his cheek.

With the cupboard hard against her back, she clung to the pie tin and tried to brace herself. He gathered her up against him, drawing her closer, smashing the pie right between them.

"Oh!" The pie tin clanged noisily to the floor. The top of the pan had been turned away from her, thank goodness. She covered her mouth to keep from laughing out loud as he took a step back and frowned down at the pie that dripped from his shirt.

He said something low and naughty, and she bit the inside of her cheek to keep from smiling. Donovan scooped up as much of the pie as he could with one hand and bent down to pick up the pie pan. He popped it back into it.

"Your shirt's a mess," she pointed out, unable to keep the giggle from her tone. He frowned down at it and then did the most horrifying thing. With the ease of a man comfortable in his own skin, he pulled the shirttails out of his pants and grabbed the bottoms. "What are you doing!" She grabbed his wrists.

"I'm taking my shirt off." He tugged the shirttail up, revealing taut skin, a sprinkling of hair, and, oh my, was that his belly button?

"You aren't wearing an undershirt." She closed her eyes tight.

25

"Yes, I am. I just grabbed it with the shirt. The pie went straight through to my skin."

She opened one eye and peeked. "You're not wearing a union jack?"

"One thing you should learn about me, darling." He pulled the shirt off with one quick overhead motion. "I don't like wool, and I'll be damned if I wear anything with a drop seat."

The moonlight shone across his wide chest. Muscles rippled, and she blinked twice before she realized that she had opened both eyes.

He looked like a Greek statue come to life. She had no idea that men actually looked like that. His skin was tan and smooth over muscle that rippled across his stomach like the ridges of a washboard. His skin looked sunkissed. She concluded that he must work outside without a shirt on. A very thin band of pale skin teased her where his waistband clung to his hips.

He paused with the shirt in hand and grinned sideways. "We could finish that kiss." He tossed the shirt down on the table next to the pie tin as if laying down a gauntlet.

"I don't think that's a good idea," she whispered.

He took two steps toward her. She ducked under him and fled to the safety of her bedroom door. When he didn't follow, she clung to the frame and looked back. He was the most beautiful half-naked man she had ever seen—okay, the only half-naked man she had ever seen—and she was alone with him.

She could not help her own reaction. Her fingers itched to touch him, to feel the muscle and bone underneath all that lovely skin. Her nose twitched at the scent of clean man and cinnamon.

"Come here," he ordered. His baritone voice caressed her ears and sent shivers through her skin.

"No." She barely got the word out.

He crossed his arms over his chest like a genie from a fairy story. His look was confident and commanding. "You know you want to."

"I know nothing of the sort." She managed to sound haughty.

"Lillian." He crooked his finger. His eyes sparkled in the

moonlight. With great effort and as much dignity as she could muster, she shut the door and turned the key, locking the wooden barrier between them.

She rested her heated forehead on the cool wood and closed her eyes, enjoying the memory of his chest burned into her eyelids.

"You can't look at me like that and lock the door between us."

She jumped at the sound of his voice. It came through the wood as if he stood with his forehead pressed on it. She took a step back. "Looks like I did," she said to the door. "So you have to deal with that."

"Oh, I'll deal with it." His tone held promise, and for some reason it made her stomach quiver and her skin feel all hot.

The doorknob rattled. The sound sent her across the room in terror and, she had to admit at least to herself, excitement. Her gaze danced about the room, landing on her dressing chair. She grabbed the chair and shoved it up under the door handle as extra protection.

Her heart raced in her chest. Her breath was fast causing her to be this side of light-headed, which made her frown. Lillian had never been the fainting kind. Why did she feel this way now?

"Here's the thing, love," he said low.

She tiptoed toward the door to hear him better. "What's 'the thing'?"

"When a woman looks at a man like you looked at me . . ."

"Yes?"

"There isn't a door or a chair or even a dresser that's going to keep him from her. Not if he's a real man."

Lillian's mouth went dry, and she swallowed hard. "Are you a real man, Donovan?"

"Honey, they don't come any more real than me."

Her palms broke out in a sweat. She paced the floor. Every nerve in her body wanted to open the door and see what would happen. Thank goodness her common sense kicked in. Good lord, she had just met the man this afternoon. She didn't know anything about him.

Except how he looked standing in her living room with his shirt in his hands. How he tasted when his lips touched hers. What his hands felt like on her waist. How his skin smelled, warmed by the sun with a hint of the barbershop shave cream.

Well, then, she did know quite a bit about him really.

He pounded on the door. "Lillian, open the door. We need to talk about this."

"No." She did the sensible thing and leaped into her bed, pulling the covers up to her chin. Her whole body quivered. But not from fear; that was the one emotion she never felt around Donovan.

"I'm warning you."

"I don't care!" she called back.

Then, with a violent bang, the door burst open. The chair splintered and fell, shooting across the floor. The door itself hit the wall and hung crookedly on its latches.

The violence of the motion should have had her cowering under her sheets, except Lillian wasn't the cowering kind. Instead, she leaped from the bed and attacked him. Running straight for him, she swung her fist, but missed. Donovan ducked and managed to dip his shoulder and pick her up.

Lillian fought him, but he had his arm banded across her thighs while his hand held her wrist. She struggled to be free, but he only adjusted her so that she hung nearly upside down on his bare back.

"Don't even think about biting me," he growled.

"Why not?" she asked. "You have all this lovely exposed skin, and I didn't get any dinner."

She felt the laughter before she heard it, pressed against strong, warm muscles. Her toes dug into the waistband of his pants, her braided hair hung beside her head, swinging.

"What, pray tell, is so funny?" she asked. "I could bite you. In fact, I should bite you."

Before she could blink, he swung her into his arms like a small baby. Shocked at being so close to the very flesh she coveted, Lillian stared at his dazzling blue eyes, the hours-old beard and roughened skin of his chin and felt something strange and wonderful. For the second time in the day, the second time in her life, she felt safe.

Which was just absurd.

The man was nearly naked and just beat his way through her bedroom door. She should be terrified. She should faint. Instead, she laughed.

Her laughter mixed with his and he carried her to the bed, tossed her down, and stood over her.

"Woman, I do declare you keep a man guessing."

"You scared me," she said when she could catch her breath. "You really shouldn't do that; it's not safe."

"It's not safe?"

"No, it's not." She shook her head solemnly. "You could get hurt."

"I could get hurt?"

"I'm giving you fair warning."

"I see." Donovan sobered. He'd kicked the door down just to prove he could. He hadn't thought about what it would be like for her, a woman all alone on the other side. Even though he knew he would never hurt her, she didn't know that. Guilt and remorse crept over him.

Damn, he'd been thinking wrong.

He crossed his arms over his chest and tilted his head. "I'm sorry I scared you. I wasn't thinking correctly."

"Apology accepted." Her voice was enticingly breathless. "Just remember, I'm dangerous when startled," she added in a barely audible tone as she scrambled to the far corner of her bed and pulled the cover over her.

"Right." He leaned against her chest of drawers. "I suppose I should be glad you didn't go for your gun."

She sat up straight and narrowed her eyes. "What did you mean by that?"

He opened his mouth and then closed it. She scrambled to her knees and put her hands on her hips, covers forgotten.

"I want to know what you meant," she said.

Oh, heck. As beautiful and compliant as she was right now, he was pretty sure she wouldn't stay that way if she found out that he'd gone through her room earlier that day. That he knew she kept a six-shooter in her dresser drawer.

"How did you know I have a gun?" she demanded, her mouth making a firm, thin line.

"I saw it." He shrugged. "Downstairs, just under the counter where you keep the ammunition you sell."

Her lovely eyes narrowed, and he didn't like how the small hairs on the back of his neck rose. Could she tell he lied?

"Hmph." She folded her arms across her chest. "I wouldn't get too sure of myself, if I were you. I'm a good shot, you know."

"I'm sure you are." He leaned over and kissed the top of her head and inhaled the lavender scent of her soap.

"You, sir, are going to repair my door."

He blew out a breath. "I think there shouldn't be any doors between a man and his wife."

"We are not married," she said as if he were slow to comprehend. "And you *will* fix my door."

"I am your husband, and I will not put doors between us." He straightened and towered over her.

"Then I'll do it myself." She lifted an eyebrow, fearless.

"You do, and I'll tear it down." He admired her gumption, but refused to back down.

"I wouldn't bother if I were you, because I'll keep putting it up." Her back was stiff, her arms crossed in defiance.

Donovan shook his head. "I'll chop it up and burn it."

"I'll get more wood and make my own."

"I hate to break it to you, darling, but unless you figure on chopping down your own trees and planing the wood yourself, you aren't going to be able to make the door."

"Why would I have to do that? I'll just go down and purchase what I need from the mill." She waved her hand toward the window.

"You can try," he said confidently. He was going to win this argument. It was imperative to his case. If he were to have the town believing they were married, there could be no locked doors between them. Besides, he didn't want her to have a place to hide any illegal activity she might be up to.

"You would tell the men at the mill not to sell me wood?"

"I'll tell them you're building a door. No man in five counties will sell you wood." He smiled down at her. "You can go to Denver, but I doubt you can get anyone to rent you a wagon." He relaxed against the doily-covered chest of drawers. "Besides, who will help me mind the store if you're gone?" He smiled at his victory. "You might as well give on this point."

She scrambled off the bed.

"Where are you going?"

"Downstairs to get the gun."

He stepped in front of her empty doorway, blocking her path. "I know having me around all the time is going to take a little getting used to, but if you follow my rules you'll find the transition pretty smooth."

"Follow your rules?" Her eyes flashed. "We'll see about that." She whirled and reached for the dresser drawer. Oh, she was a handful all right—red hair, creamy skin, passionate eyes.

"That's right." He got there first, opened the drawer, and took out her gun.

"Hey!"

"You don't need this anymore," he said as he double-checked that the cartridge was empty and stuffed the gun into the waistband of his pants.

"How did you know that was there? Give it back!"

"Rule number one, you will do what I tell you." He took a step toward her. She took a step back and glared at him. "Rule number two, no doors." He took another step, trapping her against the dresser, his arms on either side of her as he gripped the top and leaned in. "Rule number three, no guns." Her agitation showed. "Rule number four"—he eyed her soft mouth, firm and frowning—"when in doubt, refer to rule number one."

Her eyes narrowed and her mouth tightened. He knew she was about to give him what for. He could feel the tension between them soar. It was a matter of timing, really. The moment she opened her mouth, she was his. Wait for it . . .

"How dare—"

He covered her open mouth with his and dove in. She tasted of mint. Her breath was soft against his cheek. There was a brief pause as shock prevailed and then . . . oh, yes. She softened into him.

His fingers dug into the wooden dresser. His arms strained not to crowd up against her.

She made a small helpless noise in the back of her throat and wrapped her arms around his neck. Sweat popped out on his forehead as he fought a fierce battle with himself to keep a distance. This seduction was for work purposes. Not real. *For interrogation,* he told himself.

He took a step back, breaking the contact. It took every ounce of his self-control to get a grip on his raw emotion.

"Donovan?" She spoke his name softly, her tone confused and uncertain. The sound of it rasped against his heated skin.

"Yeah." He forced himself to take the steps necessary to leave the room, to leave her.

"Donovan?" This time she spoke louder, and he hated the apology he heard in it.

"Good night, Lillian," he said without looking back. He crossed into the living area, grabbed up his shirt and boots, and ducked as something *whoosh*ed by his ear. He listened grimly to the crash of porcelain on the floor. She had thrown a vase at him.

She had good aim, he noted as he watched the pieces scatter on the polished floor. It would have hit him square on the back of the head if he hadn't heard it coming.

"Horrid, rotten man!"

He glanced over his shoulder. She stood in the shattered doorway, her chest rising and falling with the force of her emotion. My God, she was the most beautiful thing he'd ever seen.

"Go to sleep," he ordered and headed for the door.

"Don't you tell me what to do!" she hollered at him. He understood the anger in her voice. Right now he was just as angry at himself.

"Rule number one!" he shouted back and stormed out, slamming the door behind him.

He'd taken her gun.

She was an idiot for not thinking to use it before he found it. How the heck did he know it was even there? She paced her room in a huff.

It probably was for the best, because if she still had it, she just might hunt him down and shoot him. In her opinion, Donovan West was a man who deserved to be shot. She didn't care if she had made him up.

Of course, what would she have told the people in town? That she'd shot her husband? That he wasn't really her husband? That she'd kissed a stranger on the street?

Darn it. The real flesh-and-blood man turned out to be a whole lot different from the one she had imagined.

Lillian paced beside her bed. Her blood was up, and she had so much energy she didn't know what to do. It was too early to go anywhere and too dark to do any work.

The infuriating man and his maddening rules had ordered her to sleep. She glanced at the tangle of sheets on her bed. As if anyone could sleep after what had happened. For that matter, what the heck *did* just happen?

She played the scene over in her mind. She'd kissed him . . . more than once. Darn it. He must think that she lacked basic morals. But then again, he was the one who kept insisting they were married, and she was very certain that married people kissed each other.

What happened between a man and a woman was no mystery to her. Growing up in an orphanage, kids talked. She had a friend or two who'd gotten pregnant and then married. She'd just sworn never to do that to herself. Especially not with a man who lied his way into her life and broke down doors. No matter how good he was at kissing.

She pressed her hands to her cheeks to try to stop the heat that memory brought. He had stopped, which meant only one thing. She probably wasn't very good at kissing and such. Not that it mattered. The last thing she needed was to be thinking about kissing when things in her life had gotten so terribly, horribly complicated.

She felt all itchy and twitchy and was as far from sleeping as she had ever been. Even food didn't sound good anymore, which was a good thing, considering the state of her pie.

Her thoughts went back to Donovan taking off his shirt. All that lovely skin and muscle. The band of white where the sun hadn't tanned him. She sighed. What was wrong with her? She acted like a moonstruck schoolgirl. One thing she'd never been was a moonstruck schoolgirl. She couldn't afford to be one now.

The man was dangerous. The state of her bedroom door was a perfect example. She should have been terrified when he pushed it in; instead, she had been thrilled.

She had to be ill. Really, it was the only thing that accounted for this silliness. She touched her forehead. Her hand trembled, but there was no sign of fever. It was hot in the room, though. She opened her window and took a deep breath of cool mountain air.

Ah. That helped. It was clear by the pinkening sky that the sun would be up soon. There was no sense in trying to sleep now. It dawned on her that Donovan had left, which was exactly what she'd hoped he'd do all night.

That meant she had her apartment to herself. Rushing out to the living room, she picked up the iron skeleton key near the door and locked it. The sound of the click was satisfying, but not for long. She eyed the door. It wasn't all that much sturdier than her bedroom door. The blasted man could probably knock it in if he wanted to. She glanced around. Only the settee was large enough to cover the door.

Darn, what was a woman to do?

He seemed to know all her secrets. How? He must be a very good snoop. Well, two can play that game.

The man obviously had a secret. Why else would he be in Silverton pretending to be her husband? She tapped her finger against her chin. All she had to do was find out his secret and he would have to leave or she would be forced into telling his secret to the entire town. She frowned. If she told his secret, he might be inclined to tell hers.

Darn it! What a mess. Clearly the man was an evil criminal. After all, he stole her livelihood, tried to seduce her, and then had the audacity to set down rules.

Now what the heck was she going to do with a man who insisted on rules? She made her own rules, always had. She knew for certain she would never, ever be able to live under someone else's rules . . . especially rules that began with rule number one.

She sniffed. Good luck enforcing that rule. The idea of Donovan enforcing his rule sent a shiver down her spine. It might be interesting to find out just how he went about doing it.

Chapter Four

Donovan stripped off his clothes and dove headfirst into the icy mountain stream. He came up gasping for air, his overheated body instantly cooled. His crazed brain was too numb to think. He forced his limbs to work, taking long strokes up and down the stream until he could no longer feel his fingers.

He got out and toweled off.

"Pretty damn early in the morning for swimming in ice melt."

Donovan scowled as his partner came trotting up on horseback. McCormick looked fresh as a darn daisy in a clean shirt, pants pressed to a crisp line, and his boots shined. McCormick stopped in front of him, leaned on his pummel, and grinned. "Rough night?"

"Whose idea was it to have me play the redhead's husband?"

McCormick smirked and got down off his horse. "I believe it was your bright idea, old man."

"Yeah, well, shoot me before I come up with another idea this bright."

"Trouble at home already?"

"She's not the Widow Blake." Donovan tossed the towel on a bush and pulled on his pants. "She's too damn innocent."

"I thought you said she was a con artist." McCormick squatted down and poked the small fire Donovan had built.

"The husband bit is definitely a con." Donovan poured himself a cup of coffee from the pot. "But she's not the usual kind of con."

"How so?" McCormick helped himself to the coffee. "A con's a con."

"Yes, but I think she came up with this as a ruse to run her own business, which is different from running a bait and switch."

"Not so different," Mac said. "She has the entire town believing she's something that she's not."

"That might be, but Lillian has this innocence about her that just doesn't fit."

"I thought you said she took down Johnson all by herself?"

"She did." Donovan settled on a rock. "The gal is quick. Almost took me out a couple of times."

"So how is that innocent?"

"She has street smarts, but no man smarts."

"What do you mean, no man smarts?"

"I swear she's never been with a man before."

Mac choked on his coffee. "A virgin con artist?"

"See, now, I know it doesn't make any sense. A woman of a certain age, pretending to be married, ought to have a certain amount of experience. But I swear it's as if she's lived with nothing but women her whole life."

"Thus the early-morning swim in ice melt."

"My toes are blue," Donovan grumbled. "I don't know how to handle her. Darn it, she should be home with her mama, not alone and running some con in a mining town full of men."

"Do you know she's alone, or are you assuming?"

"No sign she isn't alone." Donovan set his coffee aside and pulled on his socks and then shoved his feet into his boots. "When I thought up this plan, I figured she was a con artist out for whatever she could get. Then I thought she may be part of the ring. You know, like a front for laundering the fake cash. But right now, I'd eat my hat if she turns out to be more than a little lady trying to run a business by herself." He frowned and eyed his partner, regret worming through him. "I don't like taking advantage of her. It doesn't feel right."

"You knew it wasn't going to be easy when you came up with the idea." Mac settled himself down on the dry, rocky ground. "I kept an eye on the townspeople. Looks like they accepted you in the role pretty damned fast."

"They all like her," Donovan said. "They were happy to finally meet her man."

"I'm surprised she didn't have you arrested."

"There wasn't anything she could do." Donovan grinned. "The only way for her to prove I'm lying was to admit that she lied. The town won't take kindly to the fact she's been conning them for over a year."

"So you don't think she's part of the gang we're looking for?"

"No. I've given it some thought, and it doesn't add up," Donovan said. "Think about it. If she were part of the gang, someone should be playing her husband."

"Maybe she doesn't like men." Mac sipped the coffee. He made a face. "Dang, you make the worst coffee I've ever tasted."

"I make it that way on purpose."

"Why?"

"To keep marauders out of it." Donovan poured himself another cup. The small holes in the spout of the pot filtered out the bigger of the black grounds. Donovan used his teeth to sieve out the rest. "And trust me, she likes men. She just doesn't know men."

Mac took out his handkerchief and wiped his cup. "You have a problem with innocent women?"

"Only ones who throw themselves at me."

"She threw herself at you?"

"Yes and no."

"What the heck does that mean?"

"It means she wanted to, but then got scared and locked the bedroom door on me."

"Sounds sensible."

"Except I kicked the darn thing in."

Mac raised a golden eyebrow. "Were you drinking?"

"Not a drop."

"I don't get it. You're usually the one escorting little old ladies across the street, not tearing down doors to ravish innocent girls."

Donovan winced. "She dared me."

"She dared you?"

"Heck," Donovan said and threw the remains of his coffee into the fire. "It felt like a dare."

"So you kicked down the door and went in after her." Mac pursed his lips. "Why are you swimming in cold water?"

"I just met the woman."

"You white-knighted it out of there."

"What?"

"Your honor got the best of you." Mac stood up. "So what did she do when you left her?"

"She threw a vase at my head."

His friend laughed out loud. "Good for her."

"Yeah, well, I think we should drop this one and take another approach."

"Why, because you're scared of a little redheaded woman?"

"No." Donovan poked a stick into the embers. "Because I don't think it's going to work."

"Sounds like it's already working," Mac said. "Listen, following Johnson hasn't gotten us far enough or fast enough on this mission. The boss is getting upset. By playing storekeeper, you're in the perfect position to get inside information and move this along. Look, the gang won't be suspicious, and you've got a firsthand look at who's passing the phony money." Mac went over to his horse and tucked his coffee cup into his saddle-bags.

"Dadgummit."

"What?"

"You're right."

Mac grinned and climbed up in his saddle. "You know you have brilliant ideas. That's why the president puts you in charge of these operations."

"Yeah, me and my brilliant ideas." Donovan's thoughts went back to Lillian. How was he supposed to deal with all that fire and innocence?

"You're a professional," Mac said without a sympathetic bone in his body. "You'll figure out how to do your job."

"You're a lot of help."

"That's my job. Listen, I'll keep my eye on Johnson, and

there's a couple of miners looking for hired picks. I'm going to work this thing from that angle. Maybe find out if someone's buying silver on the side and see if they're passing phony currency. Meet you back here in three days." Mac turned his horse and headed back down the trail.

Lillian spent the early-morning hours restoring her apartment to order. She slapped the dust from her hands as she looked around. There was absolutely no evidence of the man who had kept her up all night. Well, except for the lack of a bedroom door, but she'd fixed that. He didn't tell her she couldn't put up a curtain. A gal's got a right to some privacy.

She'd also stashed some food in a covered cake container under her bed. She'd be darned if she were going to starve every night because of him. She'd be just as darned if she were going to make him dinner. No matter what he said, they were not married.

Lillian put a clean apron on and checked her hair in the mirror. Her gaze went to her mouth and her still slightly swollen lips. He'd kissed her. He'd kissed her good. She was filled with emotions she was still sorting out.

Desire, need, want were all wrapped up in her naturally curious nature. Heck, she'd had a taste of something last night that left her wondering. Was it like that kissing every man or just the one impersonating her husband?

She'd been kissed only once before and that was by Bobby Ray Silus. She'd been fourteen and he'd been eighteen. His kiss had been a bit sloppy and awkward as he'd banged her nose and pulled her hair. She'd decided then that it wasn't worth the bother. No matter how pretty a man was to look at.

But last night had not been awkward. Heated, yes, but not awkward. Focusing on her dreamy reflection, she frowned at her thoughts. The man had broken down her bedroom door. No telling what other dangerous things he could do . . . like tell the townspeople all her secrets.

Which he hadn't . . . yet. And that begged the question,

why not? What was he doing here besides ruining her carefully built life?

She went downstairs and opened the shop. It was eight o'clock on the dot, but she already had customers waiting outside her door.

"Morning." She turned the sign to say OPEN and let them in.

"Morning." Emma Baleworthy looked around. "I came to meet your man."

"Sorry, he's not here this morning."

"Where's he at?" Sam Martin poked around the display of canned vegetables near the door.

Emma's wide hazel eyes filled with curiosity. "I heard so much about him. I thought maybe he'd be in the store today and I could, well, meet him."

"I hope you didn't come all the way over here just to see Donovan," Lillian said with a tight smile. "He's a very busy, very married man, you know."

Emma blinked at her. "Oh, oh, no." She gave a little giggle. "I came for some material for the dance."

"Ah, Founders Day," Lillian said. "I ordered in some pretty new silks for it. Now keep in mind that Mrs. Quidly bought up a bunch already."

"I heard that the other girls are having her do their dresses," Emma said. "But I think I can do better myself, even if she is the town seamstress. I got a magazine in the mail last month, straight from Paris, with the latest fashions."

"I don't think a pretty thing like you needs to worry about fashions from Paris," Lillian said with a soft smile. "Why, the miners will be lining up in waves."

"It's not miners I'm looking to attract," Emma said. "Can you keep a secret?"

"Just a second." Lillian held up her hand to silence the girl and called out over the bolts of fabric, "Sam, you keep your hands out of that cracker barrel."

The old man jumped and flashed her a guilty look. "I was just gonna buy one."

"I need to see the penny first." Sam was a decent enough fellow, but he had a bad habit of coming into the store and leaving with at least one thing he hadn't paid for. Lillian had learned early on to keep a tab going for him. When it got over twenty dollars, she kicked him out until he paid up. Two days ago, he'd hit his limit again.

"Payday's Friday," he said. "I'll give you two pennies if you float me until then."

"Not even two pennies," she said. "You already hit your tab limit this month. Do I need to get Donovan?"

Sam shoved his hands into his pockets and scraped the toe of his shoe against the floorboards. "No. I'll be going then."

"See you Friday," Lillian called after him.

"As usual." He shot her a grin just before he pushed his way out the door.

Lillian sighed. He'd made off with a can of sardines. She shook her head. Just another thing to add to his bill.

"All right," Lillian said, turning her attention back to the seventeen-year-old Emma. "What secret?"

Emma picked through the bolts of silks and ginghams. "My brother Ralph sent word he's coming up for Founders Day."

"Ralph's the one in the army?"

"Yes." Her eyes sparkled. "He's stationed in Denver, and he's going to bring friends with him."

"Friends?"

"At least five." Emma clutched a peach silk to her breast. "Oh, think of it, Mrs. West, five officers, just like your Donovan." She held the silk up against her cheek. "Do you think this is my color?"

"Well, now that is a lovely shade of peach," Lillian said, "but if you are looking for romance . . ."

"Romance," Emma said with a sigh. "Romance with a military officer. Isn't that the best?"

Lillian had no idea. Being an orphan, all ideas of romance in her life had been washed away for the sake of survival. Her thoughts turned to Donovan. Were his kisses romance?

"Mrs. West? The color?"

"Hmmm? Oh, yes, well, with your hair and eyes, I think you'd do better with a deeper color, perhaps this royal blue." Lillian held the bolt up. The color was true and accentuated Emma's skin tone and dark blond hair. "Makes your skin look like porcelain."

"I'll take five yards!" Emma said.

"Five yards?"

"Mama gave me five dollars to get everything I need for the dress. Between you and me, I think she's hoping I snag one of those officers as well. What with Caroline and Rebecca getting old enough to think about beaus."

Lillian did some fast calculations in her head. Five dollars would make a tidy profit for the day and offset Sam's pinching ways. "Then I have some ribbon and lace that will go very nicely with this silk."

"Yes, yes, and I'll need new stockings and gloves and, if there is any money left, I'd love to try on those pretty shoes up on your shelf."

"Those shoes are two dollars." Lillian bit her bottom lip. "So it would cut into the amount of ribbon and such, but they sure would look lovely with the dress."

"Put them on Mama's tab," Emily said. "I swear she'll pay you."

Lillian's heart turned light. She may make ten dollars before lunch. "Let me get the stepladder out." The shoes were on the highest shelf for a reason. Made of soft white kid leather, they were expensive and not something to buy on impulse. She dragged the stepladder over. "Why don't you go get your mama," Lillian said. "I think if she saw how pretty the shoes go with that color silk for your dress she might be more inclined to pay."

"Good idea. She's over at the café. I'll go get her," Emma said.

Lillian's heart lifted at how quickly the girl left. It would be a very good day indeed if she got Emma's mother in here. Perhaps she'd be able to talk her into buying some new silk for herself as well.

Lillian climbed up on the top rung of the stepladder but couldn't quite reach the box that held the shoes. She stretched, balancing on the top of the ladder. Her fingertips brushed the box, pushing it farther from her reach.

Grabbing hold of the lower shelf, she balanced on the tips of her toes, stretching until she was able to snag the box between her longest fingers.

Flushed with success, she tipped back and lost her balance. The box tumbled. She wobbled. Time slowed. Her brain worked out that she was falling. She could grab hold of the lower shelf, but she knew it wasn't strong enough to hold her entire weight. Plus, it held boxes with breakables like canning jars, lamps, and other things that if broken would rob her of a full week's profit.

She took a long breath in and decided it was better to end up with a few bruises than to ruin her stock. She let herself fall.

Chapter Five

Falling backward was hardly the most graceful thing, Lillian thought as her arms flailed and she hit someone heavy and hard. The force of it knocked the breath right out of her as momentum caused whomever she hit to stagger back.

Strong, masculine arms wrapped around her. A deep, baritone *hmmph* sounded as they landed on the floor. When the dust settled, Lillian peeked out from her mangled hairdo to find herself face to chest with a man.

She blinked and looked up. His strong chin looked familiar. She couldn't see much more than his nostrils from her angle, so she moved to sit up.

He groaned as her elbow clocked him in the chin. The ladder banged down on top of her, smacking her across the back. Pain shot through her, and she gasped at the strength of it.

"Don't move," he said.

Lillian recognized Donovan's voice immediately and felt the rumble of the words in his chest on the palms of her hands. "I can't lie on top of you," she said, panicked. "It's not decent."

"Ouch." He muttered a curse. "Hold still." This time strong hands banded around her arms and held her against him.

Lillian was aware of the smell of his shirt under her nose. It smelled of sunshine and fresh air. Under that was a layer of warm male and a hint of soap.

He snagged the ladder, somehow maneuvering it off her and into the aisle. Then he sat up, drawing her across his lap. A nice-size bruise blossomed on his chin where she had elbowed him. His jaw was clenched, and there was a tiny tick in the corner. His eyes flashed what she could only describe as grumpy concern. "What the heck did you think you were doing?"

His tone got her back up. "I will not be spoken to like that."

"You will if you continue to do stupid things."

She gasped. The audacity of the man was incredible. "What I do is none of your business."

"When it comes to trying to kill yourself, it very much is my business." His tone softened. Was that real concern in his eyes?

Now she was confused. No one ever worried about her. "Why do you care if I get hurt?"

"Because."

"Because why?"

"Because you're my wife," he said firmly. "Now, are you hurt anywhere?"

Lillian blinked. He was concerned because she was his wife. The man did not make any sense at all.

"Lillian? Did you hit your head?" He ran his hands over her head looking for bumps.

"No." She closed her eyes and enjoyed the pressure of his fingers on her scalp.

"How many fingers am I holding up?"

Well, now she had to open her eyes, silly man. She blew out a long breath and studied his hand. "Three."

"Okay, okay, good."

Enough of this nonsense, she thought as she pushed his hands away. "I told you I didn't hit my head. But I think I did hit yours." She fingered the swelling bruise on his chin. He winced.

"What is going on here?" Mrs. Baleworthy, Emma's mom, asked as she came through the door. "Emma, go get Sheriff Mann, now!"

"Yes, Mama!" The wide-eyed young lady rushed out the door.

The older woman stormed over. Eyes flashing, petticoats flying, she lifted her parasol. "You, sir, unhand Mrs. West."

"It's okay." Donovan gathered Lillian tighter against him. "We're fine."

"It is not all right," Mrs. Baleworthy disagreed, her turned-up nose indignant and gray curls bouncing. "It's indecent!"

"I told you," Lillian whispered.

Mrs. Baleworthy's crisp white blouse was starched stiff over her properly proportioned pigeon breast. Her navy wool skirt swished contemptuously. "I demand to know just what is going on here!"

"I fell," Lillian said.

"She fell," Donovan said simultaneously.

"That might be, but it does not explain why you have her in your lap. Of all the indecent displays of behavior . . . Now, unhand her or I will have to use force." She raised her navy blue parasol. The white lace ribbon on it fluttered, and Donovan remembered seeing another such parasol take a man out in a nearby alley.

"Gee, who teaches you women these things?" He stood as fast as he could.

Lillian rose with him, and he kept one arm under her arms and let her feet hit the floor. She winced and slumped against him.

"You *are* hurt."

"I think I did something to my ankle." Lillian raised her skirt. Sure enough her ankle had swelled over the top of her brown leather shoe.

Donovan cursed and lifted Lillian back up in his arms. They had to get that shoe off as quickly as possible. He searched for a place to set her down. The woman—Mrs. Baleworthy, was it?—gasped at his action and squawked something about him being a beast.

Donovan ignored her and headed for the counter. Ignoring her was hard to do since the silly woman beat him about the head and shoulders with her parasol the whole way to the counter. There were some days when it was simply better not to have gotten out of bed. Oh, right, he'd never made it into bed.

Donovan gritted his teeth, set Lillian on the counter, and whirled. With a quick, efficient movement, he grabbed the parasol from the outraged woman's hands just as the door jangled open.

A very large bearlike man strode through. He had long dark hair, thick enough to cover his shoulders. His beard fuzzed out, giving the impression of a young Saint Nicholas. Only this Saint Nick had a badge on his vest and a gun in his hand.

"Stop right there!" he ordered. Donovan blew out a long breath. It would have been a sigh, except men didn't sigh. They cursed, they muttered, and they blew out long breaths, but they didn't sigh—even when times called for it.

"Put your hands in the air. Now!"

Donovan did as he was told. The young girl peered at him from behind the sheriff's back. Her wide hazel eyes filled with curiosity.

"Look, it's not what you think," Donovan began.

"Sheriff, this man accosted Mrs. West. I came in just in time. Good thing I did too. He had her on the ground and on his lap." Mrs. Baleworthy's voice was breathless at the very idea. "I sent Emma to get you right away and beat him with my parasol for good measure."

"That the parasol?" The sheriff nodded toward Donovan's hand.

"Yes." Mrs. Baleworthy marched up and grabbed it from Donovan. She swung fast and furious, hitting him square in the chest and knocking the wind out of him.

"That's enough," the sheriff said.

Donovan let momentum bend him forward. He grabbed his thighs and bent down in an attempt to breathe, but he kept his eyes open in case of an uppercut. The woman *harrumph*ed and walked over to stand beside the sheriff.

"This is all a big mistake," Lillian finally spoke up. Donovan eyed her, waiting to hear what she had to say. With his luck, she'd have him arrested right there and then as an imposter. That was, if his own guilt didn't betray him first. If he wasn't careful, he'd end up at the wrong end of a short rope.

"What do you mean?"

"I reached up to take Emma's dancing shoes off the top shelf when the ladder tipped out from under me."

"Are you all right?" The sheriff showed concern in his dark brown eyes. His gaze might be on Lillian, but Donovan noted he'd not taken his gun off him. "This man didn't push you, did he?"

"Like I said, I fell. I didn't even know Donovan was in the store except when he caught me and my momentum knocked him to the floor."

"Wait! I saw Lillian fighting to get him off her." Mrs. Bale-worthy looked from Lillian to Emma. "We walked around the corner, and I happened to glance in the window and see her struggling. Why, the proof is right there on that man's chin." She pointed, and Donovan straightened and worked his jaw.

"When we tried to get up, things got tangled," Lillian said, "and I accidently clocked him with my elbow."

"A big strapping fellow like you, and you let yourself get all beat up by this here little gal?"

"Look, she did something to her ankle." Donovan was done with the whole scene. "We need to quit messing around and get her shoe off."

"Is that right?" The sheriff moved closer. "Why didn't you say so?"

Lillian's cheeks turned a nice shade of red. "Well, I—"

"Let's see it."

She lifted her skirt high enough to reveal the top of her shoe. Donovan winced at the sight. The ankle had swollen so big they were going to have to cut her shoe off. He reached for his knife, slid the top off the sheath, and eased the knife out. He made eye contact with the sheriff, who sent him a watch-ful nod. Donovan stepped forward, took Lillian's heel in one hand, and with the other made a quick slice. The buttons popped off and pinged about the floor. Lillian winced.

Donovan kept his eyes on her face. "This is going to be un-comfortable for a moment," he said. "But things will get to feeling better once it's off."

"Just do it," Lillian said. Her blue gaze met his and held. A surge of pride filled him. She trusted him enough to let him take care of her. Any other woman would have been a mass of hysterical tears. He'd even seen his intrepid sister lose it once when she twisted her ankle. His sister's ankle hadn't been nearly as swollen either.

"Okay, on the count of three," he said. "One, two—" He pulled the shoe off with a fast motion, and Lillian inhaled sharply.

"I thought you said on three . . ." The sheriff stood just over his shoulder.

"Best to not know when it's coming," Donovan explained.

"Looks pretty bad. Mrs. Baleworthy, why don't you and Emma go get Doc."

"But—"

"I'll keep an eye on this here gentleman," Sheriff Mann said. "Doc's gonna need to see if Mrs. West broke anything. I don't think she wants to have to walk all the way over there."

The older woman sniffed and hurried out the door. The bells jangled harshly on the door as she let it bang shut.

"I can carry her," Donovan said.

"The heck you will. In fact, I think you should step back. This here is a married woman, and I don't think her husband will take kindly to you touching her."

"Um, Sheriff Mann," Emma interrupted.

"What, dear? Why didn't you go get Doc with your mama?"

"Well, I just thought you should know—"

"What, child?"

"She said his name was Donovan." Emma's wide gaze went from Lillian to Donovan. "I think he's her husband." She whispered the last part.

The sheriff pursed his lips and straightened. "Don't that beat all," he muttered. "You Donovan West?"

"Yes, sir," Donovan said. He didn't look at Lillian. Instead, he waited a heartbeat for her to denounce him.

"Oh, Mama's going to be so mad she didn't figure that out,"

Emma said. "I'll go let her know." She scooted out the door after her mother.

"Well, well, welcome to Silverton." The sheriff held out his hand. "I heard you'd come out of the woodwork."

Donovan shook the man's hand and winced at the strength in his grip.

"Finally finished your commission, I see," the sheriff mused. "A man suddenly taking an interest in town life after a year."

"Yep, did my duty to my country," Donovan said. "Now I'm taking care of my family." It was the same story he'd been spreading around town.

To make it more authentic, he let go of the sheriff's grip and patted Lillian's knee. She sent him a look that should have scorched the eyebrows right off his face. Donovan turned his attention back on the sheriff. "You can put your gun away, seeing as how you don't need to defend Lillian from her own husband."

Lillian snorted, but the big man merely tucked his gun back into his holster. "Seems like maybe I need to be protecting you from her." He nodded toward Donovan's chin.

Donovan rubbed the sore spot delicately. "Purely an accident. My gal here loves me too much to batter me." He patted Lillian's knee again.

She crossed her arms. "Please do not talk about me as if I wasn't in the room. I can hear you both just fine."

The door opened, jangling the bells that hung from the top. A short bald man appeared carrying a black bag. A gust of wind blew him in. "Someone hurt?"

Mrs. Baleworthy and Emma followed right behind him.

"Hey, Jed, come on over here," Sheriff Mann said. "Jed Jackson, this here is Donovan West, Mrs. West's husband."

Mrs. Baleworthy gasped. "Mr. West?"

"I told you," Emma said in a stage whisper.

Donovan felt some vindication at the horror in Mrs. Baleworthy's eyes.

"You should have said . . ." The older woman fumbled.

"I would have, but you didn't give me time," Donovan replied.

"Nice to finally meet you." The little man shook Donovan's hand. "Your gal has told us all about you."

"All good things, I hope." Donovan glanced at Lillian. Her eyes darkened and her lips tightened, but she kept her mouth closed.

"Yes, yes, all good things." The doctor turned his attention on Lillian. "Now, what have we here?"

"I fell," Lillian said, and Donovan could feel the embarrassment roll off her. "I think I did something to my ankle."

"It looks pretty swollen." The doctor set his bag down on the counter. He put on a pair of spectacles and glanced down at her swollen limb. The room was quiet as everyone focused on Lillian's ankle.

"I cut her shoe off," Donovan said.

"Good thinking," Doc said. "We're gonna need to take off the stocking." He glanced up at Lillian. "Those are pretty fancy stockings. I don't think you want us to cut them off."

"Oh, dear me, no, don't cut them. They are lovely," Mrs. Baleworthy said. "I'm sure she got them for her honeymoon. Didn't you, dear?"

Lillian colored a deeper shade of red and for the first time Donovan noticed the sheer black silk that covered her foot and swollen ankle and went up under her skirt. For a moment his mouth went dry as his imagination followed that stocking past shapely calf to knee and perhaps bare thigh above.

"Um, if you fellows don't mind." Donovan shouldered his way in front of the doc and the sheriff. "I'll help her with the stocking."

"Oh, right, pardon me, Mrs. West." The sheriff and the doctor turned their backs.

Donovan noted that even the ladies had moved away and pretended to browse through the bolts of cloth. He looked Lillian in the eye. "The stocking has to come off."

"I know." She clutched her skirts.

"Where's the garter?"

"Just over my knee." She bit her lip. He took it as a nervous gesture. He looked from her mouth to her eyes. Their gazes locked.

"Just do it," she said in a whisper.

She lifted her skirts high over her knee, revealing pale blue ribbon threaded through the black silk and tied with a neat bow on the inside of her thigh.

Donovan's hands shook. He ground his back teeth together in an attempt to get ahold of himself and carefully untied the ribbon. Then, with great concentration, he rolled the stocking down over the top of her knee along her bare calf.

That image had cold sweat snaking down the back of his neck. Mrs. Baleworthy coughed, and he glanced up to catch her glaring at him. It was a look that said she was the decency police and he had crossed a line.

He blocked her view with his shoulder and instead concentrated on Lillian. "Tell me if this hurts too badly."

"I will," she said.

He cupped her heel and eased the rolled silk over her swollen ankle. Lillian winced.

"Is it too tight?" he asked.

"Keep going," she said through gritted teeth.

"I can cut them."

"No, they're my best pair."

He couldn't help grinning at her vanity and wondering if she hadn't worn them for him. The thought was appealing.

The doctor cleared his throat. "Are you done?"

"All done." Donovan stepped back and let the doctor take a look.

"Did a good job on this one, young lady," the doctor said, touching the swollen ankle.

Lillian winced, and Donovan frowned. Just how much did this doctor have to touch her?

"I don't feel anything broken," Doc declared. "I'd say it was a very bad sprain."

The sheriff turned back around and whistled long and low. "That looks like it has to hurt something fierce."

Lillian adjusted her skirts to hide her ankle. "It does throb," she told the doctor.

"Well, we need to get some ice on it. Do you have anything in your cellar?"

"I've got ice stored from the blocks Ted cut this winter," Lillian said.

"Bring her up a cup of shavings," Doc ordered. Donovan frowned. How the heck was he supposed to know where the cellar was? He'd been over most of the house, but not every part.

Lillian noted his discomfort and jumped in. "Take the inside cellar entrance under the stairs. No need in advertising what stock we have down there by going through the back."

Donovan was thankful for the tip. She could have let him sweat out how to find the cellar, but she didn't. Maybe pain had gone to her head. Or maybe she had something else up her sleeve. His frown deepened.

"Bring up some extra shaving for you, West," the doc said, interrupting his thoughts. "That there bruise on your chin is going to hurt all night."

Donovan knew he had to trust her. If she were going to expose him, she'd have done it already. Right? He headed around the counter and through the back room. He found a trap door under the stairs. He pulled the door open and headed into the cool darkness of the cellar. Suspicion dogged him. He didn't like the fact that Lillian was so compliant today.

Did she wear the stockings to seduce him? If so, why? Was there something she had to hide?

All good questions, he thought as he lit the small lantern and rummaged through the cellar for a bucket and something to shave the ice. Maybe there was more to the little redhead after all.

Donovan prided himself on being a smart man. He'd do his best to keep his head on straight. Then he thought of her fine skin and shapely leg. Doubt nibbled at the back of his mind. He'd have to be on his guard when it came to Lillian. She just might have the power to pull the wool over his eyes.

Chapter Six

Lillian wanted to crawl under a rock and hide until winter or the town forgot she existed. Whichever came first.

Her ankle throbbed. The ice she had packed around it did little more than give her goosebumps. Humiliation made it throb all the worse.

How could she not be embarrassed? First of all, she was silly enough to fall off her ladder. Second, Donovan had caught her. Third, she had managed to get her ankle all messed up so that Donovan and half the town knew she had been wearing silk stockings. The kind a woman wore to catch a man's attention.

Boy, did she catch his attention. She closed her eyes and groaned at the thought. Donovan's gaze had raked her leg, heating her skin. She had enjoyed every inch his fingers took as they slid the stocking down her. But they'd had an audience. Mrs. Baleworthy had a raised eyebrow throughout the whole process. Lillian had been unable to close her eyes at the time and thoroughly enjoy the sensations pouring over her.

Finally, the thought of the sheriff and the doctor seeing her entire leg had her wanting to run and hide.

Why was it exciting for Donovan to take a peek and humiliating for other men to see?

She'd have to ponder that one. It looked like she would have plenty of time to ponder. Once Donovan brought up the bucket of shaved ice, he carried her upstairs and laid her on the settee. Doc had patched her up as best he could with bandage wraps, and he ordered ice packs to be put on for twenty minutes and off for twenty. Then he left her with a small bottle of laudanum to take away the ache.

Lillian frowned at the little brown bottle. It wouldn't take away her chagrin. Or the fact that Donovan held court downstairs in her store. Laughter rang up through the floorboards as the townspeople came in to meet Donovan and to buy whatever they needed for the next week.

It wasn't right. She should be the one laughing and helping them with their goods. She was the one who knew them. She was the one who could talk them into buying more than they intended.

At least Mrs. Baleworthy had said yes to Emma purchasing the dancing shoes and a few extra items. Maybe it was the older woman's guilt that caused her to open her purse. Maybe Lillian wasn't the only one feeling humbled. Which was just fine.

Lillian started the day with a ten-dollar sale. In any other circumstances she'd be having the best day ever. She glared at her swollen and iced ankle. Stuck and frustrated, that's how she felt. She didn't like not knowing what was going on. She kept track of inventory in her own way. He would mess that up. It would probably take her weeks to figure out what had sold from her store and if anything had been pinched.

Doc hadn't said how long she'd be laid up. Glaring at her injury wasn't making the swelling go down any faster. Darn it, she couldn't have Donovan taking over her store. She had no idea if Donovan let people negotiate down her merchandise, or whom he talked to, or what they talked about. How the heck was she supposed to figure out what he was up to if she was stuck on the settee for the next week?

She crossed her arms over her stomach and huffed, working up a full head of steam.

The door opened and Donovan came in carrying a big bowl with a ladle. "Mrs. Baleworthy brought you some chicken soup." He set the dish down on the table.

"I'm not hungry," Lillian groused.

"Well, I am." He cheerfully went to the cupboard and took

out two bowls and some silverware. Whistling, he set the table and then lifted the lid off the soup and sniffed. "Smells divine."

"Mine's better," Lillian muttered.

"What's that?"

"Nothing." She picked up the laudanum bottle and eyed the label. Donovan was beside her in a heartbeat.

"Are you in pain?"

"No." She frowned at him and put the bottle down.

"Are you sure?" He lifted up the rubber water bottle that had been filled with chipped ice and glanced at her ankle. His gaze locked with hers. "Looks pretty bad."

"It's fine." She pulled her skirt down over it so that only her toes peeked out.

"So you're going to pout about it?"

"I don't pout." No, she twitched and simmered. "Who's watching the store?"

"I closed for lunch."

"What?" Outrage rushed through her. "You can't do that. Lunchtime is when I get my best stream of customers."

"Not today." He added ice to the water bottle. "The whole town knows you twisted your ankle throwing yourself at me."

"I did not throw myself at you!" Lillian gasped at the very idea. "I fell."

"So you did," he said with a twinkle in his eye. "But the town likes good gossip, and Mrs. Baleworthy enjoyed telling the story of walking in on us and thinking you needed help all the while you couldn't keep your hands off me."

"What!" Incredulous was the least of what she felt.

"That's the story she's telling," he said with a shrug. "She likes it."

"Only to keep herself from looking silly after clocking you with her parasol and bothering the sheriff with the whole ordeal."

"The townspeople told me they could spare me an hour to come up and see that you're taken care of."

"I don't need your help, thank you very much." She inhaled sharply when he placed the water bottle back on her ankle none too gently. "I've been taking care of myself for a long time, and I think I'm pretty darn good at it."

"That's why you nearly killed yourself falling off that ladder."

"I can't talk to you." She scowled. "You counter everything I say."

"Because you're wrong, and I'm right."

Rolling her eyes, she glared at him. "Oh, sure, and everyone is going to believe that."

"They already do." His beautiful blue eyes held sympathy. It came and went in an instant. "I'm having soup and so are you." He ladled soup into a bowl and brought it to her. "If you're a good girl and eat your soup, I may just let you see the receipt book."

"Hey! It's my receipt book. You can't keep it from me."

"Didn't say I would keep it from you." He handed her a spoon. "I simply said I may let you see it. Otherwise it might just stay downstairs with the cashbox." He placed a napkin over her lap and when she didn't move, he scooped up soup and held it to her mouth.

She gave him an evil look. He lifted an eyebrow at her defiance and stood over her until she gave in and slurped the soup. It burst across her tongue in rich flavors of chicken broth, carrots, celery, and onions. Her stomach rejoiced at the nourishment, but she didn't show him that. He'd only gloat.

"Good girl." He pulled one of the spindle chairs over and adjusted the small end table to hold buttered slices of warm bread. Then he sat down and offered her a slice.

Realizing how hungry she was, she took it. Lillian refused to let the man starve her out. First she had missed dinner due to him. Then her breakfast had been cut short because she had spent the time fixing her door. Now her ankle . . . She was hungry, darn it.

He leaned back in the chair and ate soup beside her. She scowled at him awhile but when that didn't seem to bother him, she stopped and simply devoured the soup and bread.

"Nice curtain," he said, breaking the silence. "I doubt it will keep me out."

"It isn't meant to keep you out."

"I'm sorry, what was that?"

"I said the curtain isn't meant to—" The man had the audacity to grin at her. It was a sideways, knowing smile that made her stomach flip and her heart skip. "It also doesn't mean that you can sleep in my bed."

"Your bed's a bit small for me anyway." He lifted one shoulder in a shrug.

"My bed is six feet long," she protested. "I don't see any reason to find a bigger one."

"Had a man in it before?"

She gasped. "That is entirely too personal a question!"

"Is it?" He sucked on his teeth for a second. "Seems to me that that is a question for a man to ask his wife."

"Then ask your wife," she said stubbornly. "Leave me out of it."

He laughed. The sound jarred her, making her spill the soup from her spoon back into the bowl. She put her spoon down and glared at him.

He got up and padded over to the dining table and refilled his bowl. "We need a good double bed," he said. "One with a headboard to wrap your hands around."

"Why would I want to—"

"I'm surprised that no one questioned the fact that you have nothing but a small single bed up here." He sat back down, ignoring the question he'd interrupted.

"I told them we were newlyweds and that was enough explanation for anyone who wondered. Not that anyone wondered but Bill Thompson."

"Who's Bill Thompson?" He raised an eyebrow.

"The man I bought the bed from."

"Did he take the bed for a test ride?" He said it casually, but she was aghast at the question.

"What? How would I know?"

He studied her face a moment.

"Eat your soup." When she started to protest, he added, "Rule number one."

She glared at him, sopped up the last of her soup with the

bit of bread, and popped it in her mouth. Only because she was hungry.

Donovan watched her, his gaze on her mouth. Suddenly she was very aware of the shape of her own mouth. The drop of soup that clung to her lip. She sucked it in, and Donovan's blue eyes darkened to the point of black. Lillian froze like a rabbit before a predator.

His gaze remained on her mouth. "We have time, you know."

"Time?" She blinked.

"Before I reopen the store."

"Time for what?" Now she was confused.

"Time to see who's right, you or me."

"Right about what?" she asked, drawing her brows together in a confused frown.

He took her bowl and casually moved to the sink. "Whether or not we fit in the bed together."

Lillian's heart leaped smack into her throat. "Oh." Her skin felt alive and tingly all over. Was it shock or because he sure looked handsome when he made unseemly statements, especially from behind. She bit her tongue to keep from saying something stupid and provoking the man.

"Lillian?" He stood halfway between her and the door to her bedroom.

"You left me last night," she pointed out. Maybe he'd remember that he found her unattractive or whatever it was that drove him from her room.

"I've had second thoughts about that." He moved in.

"I'm injured." Nervous, she pointed toward her ankle when he loomed over her.

He picked her up with an ease no man should have. She clung to his shoulders and enjoyed being near him. The warmth and safety of his arms circled her and made her want to climb inside and never come out.

Her hands trembled; she hid it by making fists.

"I promise not to hurt you." He headed toward her curtained bedroom.

"You just want to know," she accused.

"What?"

"Whether you are right or not."

"Oh, I'm right." He was so certain of that fact, she wanted to smack him. Instead, she kept her hands fisted.

"It's really none of your business."

"What?"

"Whether or not there has ever been another man in my bed." She tried to keep her chin up and look haughty. Hard to do when a man held you like a babe in his arms and strode toward your bed.

"Well, there is one way to find out."

A knock at the door stopped him before he could get behind the curtain. Lillian could feel his heart beating against her cheek. He hadn't even kissed her and things inside her had begun to melt. Maybe if they were real quiet whoever was at the door would go away.

"Mrs. West," came the shrill call of the barber's wife. "Yoo-hoo, are you there? Jessica Baleworthy sent me up to check on you." There was more knocking. "Mrs. West?"

Lillian looked up at Donovan. He scowled at the door. The sight made her smile. Maybe he didn't find her unattractive after all.

"Come on in," Lillian called back.

Donovan glared down at her. It was too late. The door flung open, and Mrs. Huckabee walked in with a basket full of goodies.

"I brought you some bread and cheese and a pie." Mrs. Huckabee set them down on the dining room table. "I see Jessica already sent you over her soup. Good, we can't have you starving." She untied the ribbon on her bonnet and turned toward them. "Oh, oh my, are you all right?"

"I'm fine. Donovan was bringing me out to the settee." Lillian nudged him with her shoulder. "I was just telling him that I wouldn't be surprised if I had lots of visitors today. Silverton is so friendly, and you take such good care of me."

Donovan scowled.

"Are you sure," Mrs. Huckabee said, "because I can come back . . ."

"No!" Lillian flashed her eyes at Donovan. "Please stay. Donovan has to go downstairs and reopen the store anyway. I'm sick to death of myself and would love to have the company."

"Then it's settled. I'll stay." Mrs. Huckabee wandered over to the settee and rearranged the pillows. "It looks like you were sitting right here eating soup." She pointed out the empty dishes. "Are you tired? Did you need to go to bed?"

"I'm fine, really." Lillian tugged on Donovan's sleeve to get him to move toward the couch. "I thought I was tired, but now that you're here, I find I'd much rather stay up and visit."

"Are you sure?"

"I'm sure." Lillian pinched Donovan. The stubborn man hadn't moved yet. The pinch set him in motion, and he put her back down. "Thank you, darling." She faced his scorching look with a brilliant smile.

Mrs. Huckabee tucked a throw blanket over Lillian's knees and settled the ice pack back on her ankle.

"Well, ladies," Donovan said and glared down at her. Lillian innocently blinked up at him. His eyes narrowed, promising future retribution. She was not afraid. "Guess I'm heading down to the store. If you need anything, anything at all, just knock on the floor. I'll hear you."

"I will."

Donovan ducked down and planted a small kiss on her lips. Shocked to her core, Lillian touched her mouth. The kiss, stingingly short, was amazingly sweet. Then he was gone. The door closed quietly behind him. Both women stared at it for a long moment, listening to the sound of his footfalls on the stairs.

"Oh, my goodness, I can't get over what a lucky woman you are, dear." Mrs. Huckabee shook her head and picked up the last of the dishes, depositing them into the basin that served as a sink. "That is one prime example of a man."

"What does Mr. Huckabee think when he hears you talking like that?" Lillian asked.

"He doesn't think, because he doesn't hear me." Mrs. Huckabee gave a short, womanly laugh. She smoothed her hair and wiggled her eyebrows. "As you know, a woman has to have some secrets from her man or he gets bored."

She sat down on the spindle chair and pulled it closer to Lillian. "Now, tell me the truth, how are you feeling? Are you too tired? Do you need more ice? And whatever happened to your bedroom door?"

Donovan closed up shop at eight. He turned the sign around and pulled the shade down. It had been a surprisingly busy day. It seemed people were still interested in meeting him and genuinely concerned for Lillian.

The thought of her injured and dependent on him made his guilt and regret for using her sink like a heavy stone in his stomach. Maybe tomorrow he would fix a chair and footstool for Lillian down in the store so that she could visit. She had seemed pretty eager to see the barber's wife.

Of course, she might have been using it as an excuse to get rid of him. Not that she had any choice. There was something between them, and he planned on getting to the root of it this very night. Maybe if he could get her to confess to her con, he could tell her why he was really here.

He rolled his shoulders and picked up the ledger and cashbox and headed upstairs. He opened the door to find the room covered in darkness.

"Lillian?" He frowned when she didn't answer. Putting the cashbox and ledger on the table, he eyed the settee. Sure enough, she lay there outlined as shadow. "Lillian, why don't you light a lamp?"

Still no answer. Her eyes were closed. He touched her forehead. There was no fever, but she didn't even budge at his touch. "Lillian?" He jiggled her shoulder. No response.

His heartbeat kicked up, and he lit the nearby lamp. There was the bottle of laudanum and a spoon sitting next to it. He picked up the bottle and noted a portion had been used.

"Lillian!" Hunkering down next to her, he took her shoulders in his hands and tried to get her to sit up. "Lillian, wake up."

She moaned at his efforts.

"How much of that stuff did you take?" he demanded. Had she overdosed?

"What?" It was clear she tried to open her eyes, but could only look at him through slits.

"The laudanum, how much did you take?"

"I didn't take any." She closed her eyes.

"Oh no you don't." He maneuvered her to full sitting position. Her head lolled for a moment before she lifted it.

"What do you want?" It was a whiny tone that didn't do anything to ease his concern.

"I want you to wake up and tell me how much laudanum you took."

"I told you." She rested her head on the back of the couch. "I didn't take any."

"A good portion of this bottle is missing. Did you take all this?"

"I didn't . . . tea." She licked her lips. Her eyes closed, but she spoke clearer. "Mrs. Huckabee gave me two cups of tea. Practically forced it on me. Said it was good for the sprain."

"Do you think she put it in the tea?"

"Maybe." Her shoulders shrugged, but the rest of her didn't move. "I don't know. Things are fuzzy."

"Don't lay down." He looked around. Sure enough there was a teacup and saucer on the opposite end table. Donovan sniffed the cup. It smelled of tea. There was a small amount left in the bottom. He stuck his pinky in, withdrew a drop, and tasted it. It did not taste like tea. The well-meaning Mrs. Huckabee must have slipped Lillian the laudanum.

One look told him she was sound asleep sitting up. Her bare toes peeked out from under the hem of her skirt. Well. The best he could do was let her sleep off the drug.

Which meant he should put her to bed. When he picked her up, she cuddled against his heart and her hands clutched his shirt. "You smell nice," she muttered, her eyes closed.

"Thanks." He hightailed it to the bedroom. She rested against him so trustingly, clung so tightly, he wondered how he could continue to use her for his own gain.

He put her down on the small single bed. The springs creaked, and he took the time to light a second lamp. When he turned back, her hair had come loose of its moorings and splayed about her. Her face was relaxed and lovely in the lamplight, but the apron looked constricting.

She'd be more comfortable in her nightclothes.

He rolled up his sleeves. It wasn't as if he were taking advantage of her, he told himself. Merely that he wanted to make sure she got the rest she needed.

Sitting down on the bed, he pulled her up against him so that he could undo the knot that tied the back of her bib apron. Gently, he pulled it over her shoulders and tossed it on the floor. Then he pulled all the remaining pins out of her hair.

The titan silk flowed across her shoulders. The sight of it made his heart hammer in his chest, but she was innocently limp against him. Discipline had him blowing out a breath. The deep breath brought him clarity and back to the problem at hand. Her clothing. She wore a corset, which could not be comfortable at all.

He unbuttoned the back of her blouse and pulled it off. She lifted her arms drunkenly, letting them flop back down when he was done.

"How about we get you into your nightgown?"

"Okay," she replied, but did not open her eyes. Her head sank to his shoulder as he worked the side button on her skirt and with no small effort tugged the skirt off.

Now they clearly were in a compromising position, as she draped across his lap, in her petticoats and her feet bare. He glanced at her ankle. It was swollen twice the size of her other ankle and an ugly color blue.

He knew the bruise on his chin probably matched hers in color. Thank goodness she hadn't given him a black eye. The chin was hard enough to explain.

Glancing down, he brushed a long lock of hair away from

her shoulder. She wore a simple white muslin shift under her corset and at least two layers of petticoats.

His palms broke out in a sweat. "Just get the corset off her and tuck her in, old man," he said out loud. "Give yourself points later for walking away."

"Donovan?" She said his name like a question and so low he almost missed it.

"Yes, love?"

"I'm so tired."

"I know," he said. "Let's get you out of the corset and under the covers."

"Okay."

She sat up with his help and he eyed the hooks and eyes on the side of the contraption. If he had it his way, he'd simply cut the darn thing off her, but then he'd already cut her shoe. She probably wouldn't be too happy with him doing more damage to her wardrobe.

"This might take a while." He stuck his tongue between his teeth and unhooked what looked like fifty eyes.

He worked in silence.

Her hair smelled of violets. The skin on the nape of her neck was porcelain white. He brushed his thumb against it to find it smooth as his mama's fine china and warm as if it were kissed by the sun.

Groaning, he concentrated harder on the metal clasps. Finally he got the last one undone. No easy feat, as his hands started to shake halfway through. He pulled the whalebone corset off and tossed it on the floor.

She sighed, then smiled. Her eyes were still closed. It was the mysterious smile of a goddess bent on seduction.

"Donovan?"

"Yeah."

"I feel odd." She tried to lift her arm, but it flopped back down.

"It's the drug, darling."

She snuggled against his chest.

With great reluctance, he rolled her gently off him and onto her back. Reaching up, she clung to his neck, drawing him down to her. She stuck her face in the place where his shoulder met his neck.

A bead of sweat inched down the side of his face. He fisted his hands and pulled away.

Her eyes were still closed. Her smile was still mysterious. "Donovan," she whispered and laid her head back on the pillow. "I think you're so pretty. Do you like me? Even a little?"

He blew out a breath. "Yes, I like you."

"But you won't make love to me."

"What?"

"You won't make love to me." Her voice grew soft, and he had to lean in to hear her.

He drew his eyebrows together. "Do you want me to make love to you?"

"Yes," she admitted, her eyes still closed, her hands limp. "But you won't. Is it because I'm a bad kisser?"

"No." Donovan tucked her under the blankets, rolled his shoulders, and straightened. "Not because you're a bad kisser."

"Okay." She drifted off, seemingly content with his answer.

He swallowed hard and tried not to think about making love to her. He'd need to swim in some more of that ice melt if he were ever going to sleep tonight. He grimaced. It was almost as if she knew what she was doing. As if she did it to mess with his head.

Well, on purpose or not, he couldn't have it. A clear mind and strong discipline were mandatory if he were to stay on target for his investigation.

Chapter Seven

Lillian's head hurt. She closed her eyes against the pain. Her mouth was so dry her tongue felt fuzzy and her ankle throbbed.

She could feel the window light against her cheek. Based on how pale the light was, it was still early morning. Her fingers clutched sheets, so she was in her bed.

Lillian frowned. She didn't remember going to bed. Her eyes popped open when she realized she didn't have her corset on. Lifting her sheets, she looked down to see that she was dressed in her shift and petticoats.

Someone had thought enough of her to get her dress off and make her more comfortable. She prayed it had been Mrs. Huckabee. The last thing she remembered was the barber's wife offering her tea.

A snore startled her, and she jerked painfully. She was not alone.

Lillian found Donovan in the parlor wing chair. He must have brought it into the bedroom. He looked as out of place as the chair and horribly uncomfortable. His legs were sprawled out, his mouth slack-jawed, and his chin covered in dark stubble. He wore an undershirt and pants, thank goodness, but his feet were free of boots. She noted through the haze of pain that he had a hole in the bottom of his sock. Maybe she could get him to spend a quarter and buy a new pair of socks.

He snored again, and the sound rattled her back teeth. She closed her eyes and pulled her hands over her ears, groaning.

"Lillian?"

"Shhh," she said. It was hard to talk with all the cotton on her tongue.

"Are you okay?" His tone was a bit gentler.

"Pain." She gulped air.

"Where? Your ankle?"

"My head. Don't shout, don't snore, and for goodness' sake, please stop talking."

He chuckled. The deep sound vibrated through her, and she growled.

"You're hungover."

"I can't be. I don't drink." Her stomach lurched.

"It's the laudanum."

"I didn't drink any of that either," she protested as best she could in a whisper. "Could you please stop making so much noise?"

"I'm not doing anything but standing here."

Was he laughing at her? That was cruel. "You're breathing."

"So are you, thanks to me."

"What do you mean by that?" She opened one eye to scowl at him.

"I mean that I thought well enough to get that corset off you when I put you to bed last night."

"I don't remember that."

"Of course you don't, you were passed out. Completcly putty in my hands."

Putty in his hands? What had happened? She tried to remember, but her mind was a blank slate of pure pain.

"I was poisoned," she whispered and closed her eyes. "Mrs. Huckabee . . ."

"Must have thought you needed rest."

"Water." She forced herself to roll over and sit up.

"Stay put." He stopped her from standing. "I'll get you what you need."

"What I really need is for you to go away." The pounding in her head subsided a little as she stabilized. She refused to open her eyes just yet. She needed to be steady if she were going to make it across the room and out the door to the outhouse.

"I can't go away now." She could hear the grin in his statement.

Her first instinct was to roll her eyes heavenward. It was a bad instinct, as the motion caused her stomach to roll. She must have done something very bad to be cursed with this man and the unasked-for concern of the barber's wife.

"Here." He nudged her hand, and she peeked out from under her lids. He held a tin cup filled with water.

She took it from him, frowning at how her hands trembled. The tin was cool and wet against her fingers. The water tasted of tin as it washed over her dry tongue and soothed her throat. She handed the cup back to him. "More."

"Right."

He poured more water from the pitcher into the cup and handed it to her. She swallowed a second full cup and passed it back. "More."

"No more, you'll make yourself sick."

"I hate you." The words didn't have much energy to them.

"I know," he said with a soft chuckle.

"How'd you get the water so fast anyhow?"

"I went to the kitchen and got it out of the sink."

"No, you didn't. You didn't have time."

"I did so." He lifted the pitcher as if its physical presence were all the evidence he needed to prove himself right.

"And what was I doing that I didn't notice you leaving and coming back?" she demanded. The rise in her tone set her head to pounding yet again. She closed her eyes and tried to breathe shallow.

"You, love, were sitting there moaning with your eyes closed." His tone was smug. "That alone is enough to give a man ideas."

She opened one eye and frowned at him. "Keep your ideas to yourself, and I was not moaning." The sound of her own voice rattled her teeth, and she stifled another groan.

He grinned gleefully at her.

"Did I tell you that I hate you?"

"Yep."

"Well, I do. Now get out of my room." She tried to wave him off, but her arms were rubbery.

"Not until you lie back down."

"No." Her bladder protested the two cups of water she'd drunk.

"Why not?"

"Because I have to use the privy." She tried to stand, but he pushed her back down. The movement jarred her head, and she inhaled sharply. "Ouch."

"Sorry, I didn't mean to hurt you."

"Sure you did," she muttered. "Now let me up. I have to go and I don't think you want me going all over the floor."

"Go ahead," he dared her and crossed his arms. "I'd like to see it."

"I really hate you." What she hated was that she couldn't get enough emotion in her voice to be believed.

"There is no way you are going to make it down the stairs and out to the outhouse on one ankle," he gently pointed out.

Fear gripped her. "I'm not using the bedpan."

"I promise not to watch."

"No," she said as clearly as she could. "I am going to the out-house, and I don't care if I have to drag your cold dead body down the stairs with me."

"Now that is an unpleasant thought," he said.

The man needed to stop grinning and take her seriously. "I can do it," she stated.

"I have no doubt you can, but I have your gun."

"I don't need my gun," she groused. Frustration had her hands curled into fists. "I'll use my bare hands."

"How are you going to get close to me? Hmm? Hobble over?"

"I hate you." The words came out on a sigh.

"Use the bedpan."

"No."

"Come on now, that's what it's for."

He didn't have to sound so sanctimonious. "Right, and I suppose you are going to empty it for me?" There was a long moment of silence. She smiled, and it hurt only a little. "So let me go to the out."

"Fine." He sounded pained. She thought he was pained only because he'd lost the battle.

"Thank you," she said as graciously as possible and pulled herself up to standing. It was difficult to balance when all the blood rushed out of her head. Her vision went completely black. "Shoot."

"I got you." He stabilized her against him. He was warm and strong and smelled good. Darn it. Her vision cleared, and she pushed at his chest. She was not going to think about how her palm itched the moment she made contact with his cotton undershirt. How she was tempted to rub. "The smart thing would be for you to stay in bed," he said.

She looked up into his pretty eyes. "No."

"Fine, I'll carry you down." Before she could protest, he had one arm under her shoulder and the other lifting her under the knees. Her world rocked, jarring and jangling as he steadied himself against her weight. Her head throbbed. Her ankle throbbed and her stomach sloshed, threatening to lose the water she had just drunk.

"You could have warned me you were going to do that," she said through gritted teeth.

"Why? Still hungover, dear?"

"I'm not—" She clamped her mouth shut and crossed her arms under her breasts. Let him take her downstairs and outside. If he wanted to haul her around, well, she wasn't going to help.

She bumped against his chest as he walked and was forced to hold on to him to steady herself. The lean strength of his muscle and bone was warm sculpture under her palm. Emotion zinged up her arm as if she had touched fire.

"What?" he asked.

"Perhaps if you put a shirt on."

"Why? Can't keep your hands off me?" he asked smugly.

She almost said yes. Instead, she clamped her lips together. "So that people won't be scandalized," she groused. "It's bad for business."

"So you want me to put my shirt on and carry you out . . . for the good of the business?"

She swallowed hard, trying to follow what he was saying through the haze of nausea and pain. "Yes."

"All right, if you say so . . . dear." He maneuvered her so that she could rest against the wall and walked away grinning. She hated it when he called her "dear." He made it sound more like an insult than a pet name.

She closed her eyes and took a moment to breathe and take stock of her present situation. She hurt from head to toe. The drug in her veins had worn off, leaving her exhausted and fuzzy with jarring pain. Her ankle shot daggers up her leg anytime she even thought about setting her foot down.

"Here." His voice interrupted her inventory.

"What?" She opened one eye to see him holding out her robe. "Oh, thank you." He had to help her put it on, as she couldn't get her arms to move properly. There was no thought of getting dressed. It had taken all her effort to put on the robe.

"Are you all right?" he asked.

She opened her eyes and saw that he'd done as she'd asked and put on a fresh shirt. It was blue with long sleeves and a front flap that was currently unbuttoned. That left a nice portion of his chest and shoulder showing. She sighed. It was a shame to cover up the rest, but she did have a reputation. At least she'd *had* a reputation before Donovan showed up in her life.

"Lillian?"

"Yes, I'm fine," she said. "Please, let's go down."

"Okay, hang on, this might jar a bit." He swung her back up in his arms. This time, she put one arm over his shoulder and rested her head against his shirtfront. If she were going to die, she might as well do it in the comfort of a gorgeous man's arms.

When she was done, Donovan carried her back upstairs. It concerned him that this feisty gal was now pale and quiet.

"I can manage by myself if I have a cane," she said through gritted teeth.

"I don't think so." He opened the door at the top of the

stairs. The movement caused her pain. He could see it in the tightening of her jaw and the way her hands clung to his shirt. "You need to be in bed."

"Please," she whispered as he headed into the apartment. "I'm not an invalid."

"You need to rest your ankle. You're in pain."

"It's my store. I should be running it."

"Officially, it's our store," he said. "You have to trust me to run it."

"I don't know you," she said and moaned.

He let out a short bark of a laugh. "You know me well enough to make an untoward proposition at me." She stiffened in his arms.

"I would never!"

"'Fraid you did." He set her down on the settee, stretching her legs so that her ankle was propped up by a pillow. Straightening, he studied her. Her pale skin blushed at his words.

"When!" she demanded as she tucked her robe around her legs.

"Last night."

"Last night? I don't remember doing anything of the sort last night. Besides, you said I was out cold."

He hunkered down next to the settee so that he could look her in the eye. "Before you passed out, you put your hands on me and told me you wanted me to make love to you."

She opened and closed her mouth. Her lovely eyes went wide. "I—"

He put his finger on her lips to stop her silly protests. Big mistake. She went as still as a stone under him. They locked gazes, and it was all he could do to not pull her against him.

"You can trust me, Lillian," he said, his voice unnaturally low. "With all your secrets. I proved that last night." *And right now,* he thought.

Standing, he crossed his arms to put some barrier between them. "You need at least another day off your foot. You can stay in bed or on the settee. Your choice, but you are not going downstairs."

"But—"

"Rule number one." His tone and movement dismissed her protest. Picking up his boots from the corner, Donovan sat in the dining chair and pulled them on. "Settee or bed? Last chance to tell me, or I'll choose for myself."

"Settee," she said weakly.

Blue-black shadows etched under her eyes told the true story. She was exhausted and in pain. "Fine." He gave in, got up, and tucked a throw around her. "I'll send someone up with coffee and a good breakfast." He made his way to the door.

"Donovan," she said as he put his hand on the metal door-knob.

He looked at her.

"Don't ruin my business."

"You're welcome," he said sarcastically and went out the door. He'd saved her from a bad fall, stayed up the entire night to look after her, and hauled her down to the privy and all she could say was "don't ruin my business." No wonder she wasn't really married. The woman refused to give an inch.

Lillian hurt and was feeling right sorry for herself. Only two days ago she was a strong, respected woman running a good business. Now she was hurt, threatened, and dependant on a man who could very well take her livelihood away from her. The worst part was she found herself attracted to the man. Donovan West, or whatever his real name was, could very well be a dangerous criminal. She eyed her bedroom curtain and frowned. All right, so he might have broken down her door, but he hadn't hurt her . . . not really. She took a deep breath and admitted to herself that he seemed a patient soul to care for her overnight when she was vulnerable and help her even to the point of carrying her down the stairs. Still, he was invading her life. She crossed her arms over her chest and contemplated her purple toes and swollen ankle.

The real question was why? Why was he here? If he really wanted her store, he would have gone straight to the bank and sold it off for cash. The thought sent her mind whirling. He still could, now that she was an invalid. In fact, it wouldn't surprise her at all if, come the evening, her store was shuttered and the horrid man gone, along with her life's savings. She didn't want to think about what she would have to do then or even where she could possibly go. Not to the sheriff. If she told him she had lied to the town and that Donovan West or whoever he was stole from her, the man might even think she deserved it.

You can trust me with your secrets, he had said.

Lillian stared out the window at the purple mountains in the distance. She had never trusted anyone with her secrets. It was a lesson learned early on in her life at the orphanage. Why would he think she would trust him now, a total stranger? Did he really believe her to be that naive? Well, he was wrong.

She thought about what she could tell the town about him. Nothing, really; he was too handsome, too charming, and, most important, she had let him kiss her in front of witnesses. Darn it. No, no one in town would have pity on her if he sold her store and ran out on her. Not after she'd pulled the wool over their eyes for so long. Why, even Mrs. Huckabee would be shaking her head and shutting her door on Lillian. Of course, Will Stewart was looking for a wife. The thought made her grimace. No, that wouldn't work. If Donovan sold her out, she would have to leave Silverton and barter her way onto a stagecoach for somewhere big enough she could get hired as a seamstress or a washerwoman.

Sadness at the thought of starting over sat heavy in her chest, but only for a brief moment. She raised her chin and narrowed her eyes. She refused to let that happen. No, she would take control of the situation. As soon as someone came to deliver her next meal, she would set a plan into motion. What that was she had no idea, but she had a lot of time on her hands to figure stuff out.

Lillian reached into the drawer of the small table next to the settee and took out a writing box. Carefully selecting a piece of paper, she began a note to the barber's wife. If anyone could help her figure out what was going on, it was the town gossip. Lillian bit her lip. All Lillian had to do was figure out how to get Mrs. Huckabee to help without tipping her off to why she needed it.

"Put five of those pickaxes on the list," the short, dirt-covered miner said.

Donovan made a note. The miner had come in with Mc-Cormick, a new hire, to collect more equipment for the mine. Donovan had to admit that Mac was out of place. In fact, his partner was really too tall and too clean for mine work. The best miners were under five foot five. Mac pushed six foot two inches.

McCormick nodded to Donovan and picked up a fifty-pound bag of flour and hauled it to the wagon.

"New guy's kind of tall, isn't he?" Donovan asked.

There was a twinkle in the dark brown eyes of the miner. He took off his hat, which left him with a band of clean skin across his forehead, and wiped his forehead on his sleeve. "The boss said take any able-bodied men who applied. We'll find work for him to do."

Donovan leaned against the counter. "Ask me, he looks a bit like a dandy."

"Told me that he sold everything and bought a mine out here, but it was salted. Once the salted silver ran out it was useless. He can't go home with empty pockets, so he's willin' to work."

"Let me guess," Donovan said. "You'll be having him haul supplies every week."

The old miner grinned. There was a gap in his smile where a tooth used to be. "We're going to see if he can cook."

Mac stepped through the doors, and Donovan straightened. "That's fifty pounds of flour, twenty pounds of sugar, fifty pounds of beans, two slabs of salt pork, five picks, and two boxes of bullets. You boys expectin' trouble?"

"Nah, just preparin'," the miner said. "Say, heard your missus hurt herself. How's she doin'?"

"She's not happy."

The old man chuckled. "She's a fighter. I bet she'll be down here and into the business by tomorra."

"Good thing I'm not a betting man," Donovan said. "I'm thinking you'd win that bet."

"Okay, put all that on the mine's tab." The old man pulled a crumpled bill from his pocket. "I want some of that cinnamon candy."

"How much?" Donovan asked.

"Well now, yer wife usually gives me a baker's dozen."

"So, thirteen?"

"Yeah."

"That will be twelve cents." Donovan handed the sacked candy to the miner. Mac had his hands in his pocket and his eye on the street. Donovan narrowed his eyes when the old man reached back into his pocket. What Donovan wanted was that crumpled bill, not coin. They were looking for counterfeit paper.

The miner pulled some change out of his pocket and pushed it around. "Well, it looks like you're going to have to give me change."

"No trouble." Donovan was happy to get his hands on the note. He took it and opened the cashbox, counting out the old man's change. The miner put his hat back on and moved toward the door. Donovan picked up the bill and noted Mac eyeing him. Donovan shrugged. His partner followed the old guy out the door.

Donovan studied the money. It looked genuine enough. He put it in the cashbox with the others. So far he hadn't seen a single counterfeit piece. Maybe they were in the wrong place after all, he thought as he glanced up at the ceiling. Mrs. Huckabee had come down and apologized for drugging his wife and told him Lillian was asleep. He had a strong urge to go check on her, but he knew better. Whenever he was around her all thoughts of his mission died. It was like setting tinder next to a roaring flame.

He put the cashbox down under the counter. They'd better find the counterfeit ring soon or things were going to get complicated fast.

Chapter Eight

Lillian fumed all day. She hated the fact that she was stuck upstairs while Donovan ran her business. Two days now and he was probably mucking up her ledger and her accounts.

Meanwhile, it had taken the better part of the day to clear her fuzzy head. Now all she wanted was a bath, some clean clothes, and a good meal. She'd been short on all three since Donovan showed up.

The wretched man waited until after eight P.M. to come up and face her. He walked in and shut the door.

The sight of him made her heart race. She took a deep breath.

"Where have you been?" She winced at how wifelike that sounded.

Donovan put his hat on the small table by the door and sat down to pull off his boots.

"Hello to you too," he said. "We've had quite a few sales in the last two days. I didn't like the idea of all that cash hanging around, so I took the cashbox over to the bank."

"How much cash?"

"Enough. I met Mr. Sandler, the banker. I had him put it in our account."

"You mean my account."

"Our account." The infuriating man leaned back in his chair and his eyes glittered. "He said his bank guarantees the accounts are backed with real federal gold."

"No one's ever had a problem with the bank." Lillian cocked her head. "Why? Are you looking for trouble?"

"Just protecting what's mine." He got up.

"You mean what's mine," she corrected him.

"Ours." He poured wash water into the basin and washed his hands. "We make a pretty nice living." He dried his hands on a towel.

"Is that why you're here?" she asked.

"Is what why?"

"The money." She let her tone rise. "Is that what you want? I may have enough to make you go away if money is all you want."

He stalked over, put one hand on either side of her head, and bent down so that they were nearly nose to nose. Lillian pushed back against her pillow in self-defense. "No, love," he said, his mouth hovering above hers. His breath smelled of mint. His eyes were so close she could see flakes of navy in them. Her body reacted to his closeness by trembling. Heart racing, it was all she could do not to draw his mouth down to hers. "I'm not here for your money."

"Then what are you here for?" The words came out just above a whisper. His skin smelled like bay rum. She noted he'd shaved since she saw him this morning.

His gaze ran a heated path over her face and lingered on her lips. She fought the urge to reach up and push her fingers through his thick hair, drawing him down to her.

"To torment you." He pushed away from her.

Lillian hated the disappointment that ran rampant through her. She pulled the edges of her robe together. "Well, you're doing a good job."

"Hope you had a good visit with Mrs. Baleworthy and Emma. They tell me you're doing better." He walked over to the window and stared out at the darkening sky. "Doc says you can come down in a couple of days."

"A couple of—" She bit off her exclamation when he stared at her. His look brooked no disobedience. "Let me guess, rule number one."

"Now you're learning."

She seethed at the frustrating situation. "Have I told you how much I hate you?"

"Not since this morning," he said. "But a man doesn't forget something like that."

Lillian studied him. It was clear this wasn't working. There had to be another way to get around the man. Time to try a more feminine tactic. She closed her eyes and allowed tears to form. "I'm sorry," she whispered.

"What?" He seemed confused. "Are you crying?"

"No." She sniffed and pulled a handkerchief out of the sleeve of her robe and dabbed at her nose.

"Ah, now, there's no crying." He paced in front of her. "What is it? Does your ankle hurt? Did I say something stupid? What?"

"It's nothing." She let out a small sob and faced the back of the settee.

He muttered something vile under his breath and hunkered down beside her. "Look, just tell me what I can do . . . besides go away. I'm here to stay."

Tears glistened in her eyes. "It's just all so unexpected." She hiccupped. "You show up out of thin air and take over my life, and then I hurt my ankle and I'm stuck up here. I haven't eaten proper in days. I need a bath, and I need to go outside." She allowed her voice to rise. "I can't even go outside by myself." She covered her face with her hands.

He seemed to think things over. "Fine," he said. "I'll take you downstairs to the outhouse. Then how about I get us some supper from the café?"

"Okay." She blew her nose. "What about the bath?"

That thought seemed to cause him some concern. She peeked at him through her fingers. He was scowling. Had she pushed him too far?

"Great, fine," he muttered. "I'll haul up some water so you can take a bath."

"Thank you," she said.

"You're welcome." He picked her up. "This calls for another rule."

She put her arms around his neck and clung to him as he made his way out the door and down the stairs. "Another rule?"

"Yeah, rule number three."

"You mean five."

"No more making passes at me."

Indignant, she straightened her back and forgot her ploy. "What? I never—"

He looked down at her. She narrowed her eyes and decided she should give him what he wanted. Lull him into complacency. "Fine, but you'll have to leave the apartment when I bathe." She paused. "Otherwise, who knows what might happen when I'm naked."

He nearly fell down the last stair. She bit her lip to keep from grinning. Oh, things were going to get very interesting very fast.

Donovan crossed the street like a man on fire. He'd filled the tiny bathtub with water, left the bar of soap and a towel nearby, and then, after checking that she had everything she needed within reach, he hightailed it out of the building.

What possessed him to tell her he'd draw her a bath? It had to be the tears. Damned if he wasn't a sucker for tears. It was something his sister had figured out real fast. Even when logic told him she was faking, he still couldn't say no to tears.

If he were a drinking man, he'd be headed to the saloon. But he wasn't. Besides, Lillian had told the town her husband didn't drink. It was how she had gotten away with him never being at the saloon. If he went in now, people might get suspicious.

A man emerged from the shadow of the café's false front porch. Donovan stopped cold, and his hand went to the gun that rested on his left hip.

"You Donovan West?"

Donovan narrowed his eyes. "Who wants to know?"

Bart Johnson stepped out into the light from the café window. "The name's Johnson, and I'm finding it mighty suspicious that you showed up after so many months."

"I've been completing my commission." Donovan's hand rested comfortably on the butt of his gun. "But that doesn't mean I haven't been around long enough to know some things about you."

"Ain't nothing to know." Bart spit on the ground. "'Cept that I think you're a fraud."

"Mister, are you calling me a liar?"

"I'm sayin' a man's got to be crazy or lyin' if he leaves a woman alone for as long as you did." He spit again. "You don't look crazy to me."

"Now, why would I lie?" Donovan stepped toward Johnson. "Furthermore, why would Lillian lie?"

"I don't know what you're up to"—Johnson held his ground while Donovan stopped inches in front of him—"but I'm keeping my eye on you."

"I'd be keeping my eye on the law if I were you, mister," Donovan said. "I heard Sheriff Mann doesn't take kindly to men who accost women in alleys."

"She tell you that?"

"Lillian's my wife. She tells me everything." Donovan allowed a glimpse of his anger to show in his gaze. "You touch her again and you're a dead man."

"You think you can hurt me? Ha! I've got friends more important than you, Mr. West, or whoever you really are." He shrugged into his long wool coat. "You and your little lady better remember that."

He pushed past Donovan so their shoulders hit. Donovan allowed the motion to turn him. A smart man wouldn't turn his back on a snake like Bart Johnson.

"Remember that, Mister supposed-to-be West." Johnson sneered. "I got friends."

Donovan took his hand off his gun when Bart sauntered down an alley away from the main street. So Bart Johnson suspected he wasn't Donovan West. Donovan looked around the dark empty streets. That meant that there were other people who might suspect the same thing. He'd have to work on that. Blowing his cover could jeopardize the case, or worse, get Lillian hurt.

There was very little time to cement his friendship with the other shop owners. He'd have to work on that. In the meantime, he'd ask around and see what they thought of Bart Johnson and his so-called friends.

It felt so good to be clean. Lillian sighed and ran her brush through her hair. She sat next the open window, and the cooling breeze off the mountains helped to dry her hair.

What an arduous task that had been. Getting in and out of a tub full of water was incredibly difficult. Thank goodness Donovan had agreed to be gone. She wasn't sure how she would have managed it with him in the house, knowing that they were separated by only the thin curtain she put up over her doorway.

She looked down at her ankle. It was turning a lovely shade of yellow green. The swelling was down a bit. Testing the skin with a poke caused her to wince. Still, she hadn't let it hamper her from putting on a clean nightgown and her robe.

Her stomach rumbled. It had been a while since she'd eaten a full meal. She wondered when Donovan would get back. The hurricane lamp in the window beside her flickered in the breeze. Between her ankle and the laudanum Mrs. Huckabee had slipped her, she had been completely thrown off her game. Somehow Donovan had insinuated himself into her life to the point where he felt comfortable depositing the week's profits in her bank account.

A frown marred her face. That was not good. He said he hadn't shown up to take her money. For that matter, the perfect time to do so would have been while she was drugged and hurt. So then why show up in Silverton and pretend to be her husband? So far the gossips had discovered nothing else new in town, which left Lillian shaking her head and wondering what was in it for him.

There was nothing in it for her. The man had control of all her finances and, if she heard him correctly, he had complete control over her.

"Ha!" she said to the room. "Rule number one, my eye." So what did she know about him? He knew how to take care of her, even if he grumbled while doing it. A single look from him could cause her body to melt into a pool of lamp wax. Darn it, he smelled good.

Anything a man and his wife do in the privacy of their home is decent. Donovan's words from their first night together floated through her mind. She had imagined she could seduce him and discover his purpose, but then her foot had gotten in the way. When she mentioned being naked in the tub, he'd headed out the door faster than you could make a dog chase after a bone. That meant her seduction plan wasn't working very well.

She pursed her lips and tapped her brush on her chin. Why? Why wasn't the seduction working? The man could seduce her with the crook of his finger. Shouldn't she be able to do the same?

Then again, maybe it was working. Didn't he make up some silly rule about not making a pass at him? Perhaps he was more susceptible than she realized.

The downstairs door opened and closed. Donovan came up the stairs. She decided to test her theory and adjusted the blankets so that her injured ankle was raised up, leaving her leg bare to the knee.

The door opened with a bang. "Too bad if you're not decent," his voice projected from behind three boxes. "I've brought a full dinner." He kicked the door closed and then walked over to the table, setting the boxes down.

"What did you bring?" she asked, her curiosity up.

"Three courses." He unstacked the boxes with pride. "Soup, roast beef with potatoes, gravy, and beans, and then dessert."

"What kind of dessert?"

"Peach pie . . ." He glanced her way and froze when he took in her exposed flesh.

His reaction had her heart pounding in her throat. She fought the urge to cover her leg. "Peach?" she squeaked.

"Pie," he added after a brief moment. Then he frowned and turned back to the table. "Evie sends her regards."

"Oh, thanks." Lillian put her brush down on the table and

debated leaving her leg exposed. Probably not such a good idea. She already knew he wasn't impervious to her. She adjusted her blanket. "Do you want me to come over to the table?"

He cleared his throat and made a production out of unboxing the food and setting it out. "No, I'll fix you a tray."

She liked the hum of tension that filled the room. She was certain now that he was as aware of her as she was of him. The fact that she was in her nightclothes and they were alone together added to the mix.

It was a pleasure to watch him. The man moved with unusual grace for his size. Stopping at one point, he took off his jacket, hanging it over the back of one of the dining chairs. Then he ladled soup into bowls and prepared the tray.

She noted the way his crisp cotton shirt moved with him, revealing and concealing the solid muscle underneath . . . the sprinkle of hair on his forearms where he'd turned up his sleeves before he spooned gravy on mashed potatoes . . . the ease with which he wore the gun that sat on his left hip.

Her eyes were drawn to the tie that held the holster to his thigh. She'd never seen him without his pants on.

He turned with the tray in hand just as she had that thought and stopped cold. She glanced up. He seemed to have known what she was thinking. His eyes darkened and his jaw clenched. It was enough to send her heart into overdrive.

"I thought you were hungry," he said in a near growl.

"I am."

"For food." He did not move.

She tipped her head to the side. "What else would I be hungry for?" His gaze narrowed, and she kept very still. In a way it was like teasing a mountain lion, thrilling, breathtaking, and dangerously stupid.

"Lillian . . ."

"Yes, Donovan?" She noted how his knuckles turned white as he clenched the tray.

"You're playing a very dangerous game."

Her mouth went dry as dust. "What do you mean?"

"You know what I mean," he said low enough to make gooseflesh rise up on her skin. "You continue this, and I am not going to be responsible for what happens."

She blinked at him. "You mean my dinner getting cold?"

He closed his eyes, took a deep breath, and seemed to have to work hard at getting control of himself. It made her smile. He opened his eyes, and she wiped the smile off her face. "It smells good."

He took the few steps toward her and thrust the tray into her hands and then whirled and headed out of the house. The bang of the door behind him was followed by his footsteps on the stairs. She winced when the outside door banged closed as well.

Eyeing her tray, she picked up her spoon and tasted the soup. So the man did have weaknesses—tears and desire. She felt better about her situation already. Whatever battles he fought with himself were no match for her own ingenuity.

Suddenly she was certain it wouldn't be long before she knew everything there was to know about Donovan West, including his real name and why he was in Silverton.

Another sleepless night and Donovan was grumpier than a bear. He unboxed a carton of canned vegetables the train had brought in and tried not to let his mood show on his face. The last thing he wanted was the people of Silverton to start speculating that there was something wrong.

"Hey, Donovan, how's the missus?"

"She's sleeping, last I checked on her," he replied. It was the same question every time someone new stepped through the door of the market. Other than the lack of sleep, Donovan decided it was a comfortable thing, running a small business like this in a town like Silverton. The people were friendly enough, and due to the success of the silver mines, the goods flowed out of the store at a pace he would never have believed.

No wonder Lillian wanted this life so badly that she'd lied to get it.

His thoughts went to the woman upstairs. Being confined to the apartment drove her mad. He almost felt sorry for her, but in a way the accident had been the best thing that could have happened for them both.

Besides putting much-needed distance between them, it gave him the opportunity to establish his presence in the town. In a few short days he'd become friends with Ed Huckabee, the barber who owned the building across the alley, and Art Miller, who owned the feed store.

It also gave him the opportunity to go through her books. She kept a steady ledger. Some families ran tabs and paid with venison, extra lard, and produce, as well as pies or cakes. Others paid in pure silver. Then there were those who paid in U.S. dollars. It was that group that interested Donovan the most. They were the group who either would be part of the counterfeit ring or were in some way duped by it.

He made a list of the folks who paid in cash over the last year, and then he made it his mission to get to know the people well. If they were on a friendly basis, then no one would be suspicious if he asked questions about where they got their paper money.

To distract himself from thinking about a certain redhead, Donovan wondered how Mac was doing. He heard through the grapevine that the new hire out at the Colbert mine had impressed the men with how much ore he could dig out of the earth. Sounds like Mac was having an easier time with his cover.

It was Friday and word was the mining crews would get paid today. He kept an eye out for his partner when the wagons pulled in and the dirt-covered miners got out.

"They'll hit the bathhouse first," Lillian said behind him.

Donovan scowled at her. "How did you get down those stairs?"

"I walked." She lifted her right hand and showed off a cherry wood cane with a lovely silver top.

"Where'd you get that?"

"Don't think you can take it away." She hobbled slowly through the doorway to the stool behind the counter. "There are others where this one came from."

"Where do you get this stuff?"

"I own a store, remember?"

"You mean we own a store."

"It's going to get very busy in here in about five minutes," she said absently as she watched the men abandon the mining wagons like ants crawling out of an anthill. "I am assuming you filled out the supply orders the way I told you. Otherwise we might run out of things and that could get ugly."

"What do you mean by ugly?" Donovan crossed his arms and leaned against the wall. "Should I unlatch my gun?"

"I don't know." She calmly settled her skirts. "Do you need a gun to settle disputes?"

For a second his traitorous mind remembered how she'd been eyeing his holster the night before. He straightened to take a step toward her when the door jangled open and ten men in dirty work boots and even dirtier clothing stomped inside. They were loud and demanding. Donovan had his hands full filling orders while Lillian sat with the ledger and cashbox on her lap.

After two hours of constant activity, the crowd in the store had dwindled down to four or five men who were in no hurry to leave. Two pulled up barrels and laid out a board near the window and played a loud and thumping round of checkers.

Donovan kept his eye on the three other men. It seemed at least one in every ten men tried to walk out with something without paying. For some, all he had to do was stop them at the door and silently point the way to the cashbox. Others were belligerent, and Donovan enjoyed kicking their sorry dirt-covered butts back out into the street. It felt good to use his muscles again.

Outside, the streets were filled with men with full pockets and not a lot of sense in their heads. He was glad he was there to protect Lillian. He didn't like the thought of her all alone on nights like this. Even a hound dog could tell it wasn't safe.

He didn't care how well she handled that man in the alley. This many men were a danger to any person walking alone. Funny, he hadn't thought about it when he'd come into town following Bart Johnson.

He glanced at the beautiful redhead and understood why it was different now. Now he had a stake in the town, a stake in the store. For his mission, of course. He shook any other thoughts from his head.

The doorbells jangled and a big burly miner stepped inside. Water sloshed off his hair and beard from the bath he had taken. His clothes were damp, but still dirty. Seems he'd bathed and put his dirty clothes back on without a second thought.

"Where's my Lilly?" His voice rattled the rafters.

"Hey, Bruce." Lillian smiled. "How's my favorite miner?"

The big man stormed his way past Donovan, picked up Lillian, and twirled her around in a bear hug. Then he proceeded to kiss both of her cheeks. Donovan cleared his throat when the man got close to kissing her full on the mouth.

"I wouldn't be doing that if I were you." Donovan put his hand on the hilt of his gun.

The big man turned with Lillian in his arms. "And who's to say I can't kiss my favorite flower?"

"I do." Donovan's blood was up. No man should be holding Lillian like that but him.

"Bruce," Lillian said. "This is Donovan West. Donovan, my good friend, Bruce Pawtauk."

"Donovan West, Donovan West," Bruce muttered absently. "Should I know that name?"

"You should." Donovan took a step forward, unable to tell if the guy was dense or kidding. "Now, put down my wife before I have to make you put her down."

"Your wife?" Bruce looked from him to her with false and, as far as Donovan was concerned, over-the-top amazement. "This guy is *the* Donovan West? Your husband?"

"That's right, and I told you to put her down." Donovan fisted his hands and rolled to the balls of his feet. Emotion pushed through him that he didn't want to put a name to.

"Should I be putting you down then?" Bruce asked Lillian with a fat, lazy grin on his face.

She studied Donovan with a thoughtful look in her eye.

"Yes, Bruce, please, before Donovan gets hurt. The last thing I need is to have to take care of a stupid man right now."

"What do you mean? The last thing you need?" Bruce set her back down on her chair. "Is that cane yours? What happened?" He whirled on Donovan faster than Donovan could react. "Did he hurt you?" He poked Donovan in the chest with a fat index finger. The motion stole Donovan's breath and pushed him two steps back. He responded with a quick jab to the monster's jaw. Pawtauk's head rocked back, but the man simply shook it off and took a threatening step forward. Donovan's knuckles pounded with pain from the encounter.

"He didn't do anything." Lillian stuck her cane between them. "I fell reaching for a shoe box on the top shelf."

Bruce sent Donovan an ugly look and then turned his attention to Lillian. "Did you break anything, darling?"

"No, just hurt my pride more than anything." Lillian sighed. "Thanks."

"Not a problem." To Donovan's consternation, Bruce kept his bulk between Donovan and Lillian. "That's what I'm here for."

"What are you here for? What does that mean?" Donovan asked Lillian.

"Donovan, Bruce comes every Friday and sees that the rowdies stay outside the store."

"He does?" Donovan didn't like the sound of that.

"I do." Bruce sent him a look daring him to protest. "Miss Lilly asked me the first week she set up shop by herself. Being as you were gone an' all. I've been coming here every week since and seeing that she comes to no harm." He narrowed his eyes at Donovan. "Seems to me it's a sorry day when a man leaves his wife to fend for herself for over a year on nights like tonight. So, I agreed."

"Well, I'm here now, and we don't need your services any longer." Donovan walked around the counter to put himself beside Lillian. "Do we, dear?"

"Bruce stays," Lillian said without looking at Donovan.

"I think—"

"He stays," Lillian interrupted him. "Remember, love?" The last word was drawled and might have sounded like it had meaning if Donovan hadn't heard the undercurrent of sarcasm. "We talked about this last night over dinner?"

Donovan narrowed his eyes. What game was she playing now? "Right, and we decided we'd keep him on because . . ."

"Because you owed him after being absent for so long," Lillian replied. "And because just the sight of Bruce is enough to keep the drunks away from the doors."

"And the sight of me won't?"

Bruce laughed, and Donovan didn't like the sound. "Son, you might be pretty, but you're no match for a drunken crowd."

"Pretty?"

"He took away my gun," Lillian tattled.

The big miner shook his head. "Now, how's a gal supposed to protect herself without a gun?"

"That's what she has a husband for." Donovan's tone was as stubborn as he felt.

"Well, we'll see about that, now, won't we?" Bruce chuckled. "Excuse me a minute, darling. I'm going to go over and watch Fred beat the tar out of Henry."

Donovan waited until Bruce stood beside the men playing checkers. Then he put both hands on Lillian's chair back and turned her to face him. "I think we need to talk."

Chapter Nine

Lillian bit her bottom lip to keep from laughing at Donovan. Clearly, he was upset that she hadn't told him about her hired help, but then again he hadn't asked.

"I think you should go back upstairs." Donovan loomed.

"The store doesn't close for another two hours."

He had a determined look in his eye. "I can take care of it."

"Things are different on a Friday." She tilted her head. "If you had been here longer than a week, you'd know." His eyes narrowed, and she poked at him. "If you'd taken a moment to ask me about it, you'd know."

He hunkered down in front of her, his expression stern. "You have to start talking to me, Lillian."

"Why? Are you afraid people won't believe you're my husband?"

"No." He ran his hand over his face. "People believe I'm your husband."

"Then what's the problem?" Eyebrows raised, she waited to hear what he would say.

"Lillian."

"Yes?"

"Fine. I'm asking you about the store."

"What about the store?" Oh, she was going to make him work for this. He'd been so busy pretending all week that he knew what he was doing, it was good to finally have him asking her for something, anything.

"What exactly do you do on the weekends when the miners come into town?"

"Well, Bruce comes in around six, like he did tonight. Before six, it's pretty much busy, like you saw, but not too rowdy."

"After six?"

"After six the men have had a few hours to drink away their week's money. Then things get interesting."

"How interesting?"

"They have been known to mob the store," she said. "That's why I hired Bruce."

Silent, he thought about what she said. "Is Bruce the only one, or are there other men coming in?"

"No, pretty much it's Bruce and me. We close at eight P.M. and shutter the windows. I learned that after the first weekend, when they tossed rocks through the glass and stole anything they could reach."

"Jeez," Donovan muttered. "And you were here alone?"

"I had my gun." She'd always been alone. It was part and parcel of being an orphan; no one looked out for you but you. Yes, if anyone asked her, she was scared sometimes, but a body did what a body had to do to protect herself and her dreams. "That's what we do."

"What?"

"After we shutter the place, Bruce sits out front with a couple of shotguns full of buckshot. It's just enough to sting real bad, but not really hurt anyone as long as they don't get too close. Bruce makes sure they don't get too close."

"Where are you?"

"I bunk in the back room on Fridays and Saturdays. I keep my gun with me in case anyone gets any ideas about coming in the back door or through the cellar."

Donovan muttered something very dark and very vicious. "What the heck are you doing?"

"Excuse me?"

"A woman as beautiful as you alone with nothing but half an inch of wooden door between her and a drunken mob?"

"To begin with, the back door is two inches thick," she said. "The drunken mob usually lasts only an hour or so after the saloons shut down." She stopped, struck by his exact words. "You think I'm beautiful?"

No one had ever told her she was beautiful. Well, not like it mattered anyway. Mostly they told her she had gumption or spunk. They prided her on the way she took care of herself, but no one told her she was beautiful like they do other women. Women who were taken care of by men.

"Of course I think you're beautiful." His eyelids narrowed. It seemed he was still upset over the rough-and-ready nature of the town on the weekends. "Why do you think we're married?"

"Why are we married?" Had he gotten caught up in her story? Did he think they were really husband and wife?

"What?"

"I asked why we were married." It was a pretty reasonable question, considering. Perhaps she could catch him off guard, and he'd tell her why he was in Silverton.

"Oh . . . right." He stood. "We're married because you are beautiful and I want you, silly." Reaching out, he ran a finger along the side of her cheek. "Plus, I need you."

"You mean you need my store."

"No." He had an odd expression on his face. "I need you."

Before she could ask him what the heck he meant by all that, the doorbells jangled and a tall handsome stranger strode in. He took off his hat, and Lillian recognized him as the man from the barbershop. Even with his face covered with mining dust, he was close to the most handsome man she had ever seen . . . next to Donovan.

She glanced at her husband, who stood when the stranger entered the shop. She looked from one man to the other. They had made eye contact and appeared to be talking without saying a word.

The hairs on the back of her neck stood up. "Do you know him?"

"Yeah," Donovan said. "Stay here. I'll be right back."

Curiosity, that's what filled her, plain and simple. Here was someone Donovan knew. In fact, he knew him well enough that they could say stuff with their eyes. That meant he'd known him a long time and probably felt like they were brothers.

Maybe they *were* brothers. She sighed, just a little. Why couldn't the handsome, agreeable-looking guy have pretended to be Donovan?

Her heart told her the answer to that straightaway. She would have never kissed this second man on the street willy-nilly. People would have believed her when she denied he was her husband. He was simply too pretty to be a store owner. In fact, he was too pretty to be a miner too.

She narrowed her eyes and noted how Donovan had turned so his wide shoulders blocked her view of their conversation. Just who the heck were these guys, and why were they pretending to be people they clearly weren't?

Since Donovan wasn't going to tell her, maybe this other guy would. He looked like the weaker link. She grabbed her cane and hobbled her way across the floor.

"I haven't seen the likes of this since we were in Dodge City." The stranger glanced her way and his smiled widened.

Lillian smiled her prettiest for the handsome man. He took off his hat, leaving a ring of clean skin and his lovely blond hair free.

"Hello," he said. "I know you."

"Hi," Lillian replied. "I'm Lillian West. We met at the barbershop."

"Pleasure to see you again, ma'am," he said. "Kane McCormick at your service. I'd offer you my hand, but I still need to hit the baths."

"Kane," she said, playing with the sound of his name. "That's an unusual name."

"My grandfather had a sugar plantation."

"So you were named after sugarcane? How sweet."

He took a step closer. "No, I was named after my father. He was the one named after sugar. My grandmother had a sense of humor."

"I think I like her."

"I'm sure you would." He didn't take his sparkling green

eyes from her. She liked the attention. She caught herself wondering if she kissed him, would the world catch fire like it did when she kissed Donovan?

"I think you're close enough to my wife." Donovan put his hand on the man's chest and pushed him half a foot back.

"Ah, so, this lovely woman is your wife," Kane said.

"Only because I didn't meet you first." She sent him a flirty smile.

"Donovan is a little quicker on the draw than I am," he said. "Much to my chagrin."

"Being quick on the draw isn't always such a good thing," she said, tongue in cheek.

"I keep telling him that, but he doesn't believe me," Kane chuckled. "Maybe you can teach him the pleasure of slowing down a bit."

"I'm not sure he has that kind of time," she replied.

"I'm just fine as I am." Donovan glared at Kane. "Lillian, go sit down before you hurt your ankle even worse."

"My ankle is just fine," Lillian said. "Mr. McCormick—"

"Please, call me Kane."

"Kane, I had no idea Donovan knew anyone in town. How long have you two been friends?"

"We've known each other since we were small boys," Kane said. "Our daddies were like brothers. In fact, there was hope at one point that Donovan would marry my sister and make us real brothers."

"Really? What happened?" She was curious now. Was this man who was pretending to be her husband already married?

"I'm afraid Donovan fell for another pretty face."

"Oh, dear, so there were two women before me?"

"I believe he was talking about you." Donovan took her by the elbow and helped her back to her chair.

"Now, neither of us believes that, do we?" She sat down. "Really, tell me. Why are you doing this?"

"I told you," he said. "I need you."

"You need me?" She squashed the small thrill that went through her at the idea. "Why?"

"Doesn't matter," he said. "Stay here. I'm going to see if Mac won't help us protect the place tonight."

"We don't need any more help."

"Yes, we do," he said firmly. "You are not sleeping in the back room tonight."

"Because you have my gun?"

"Because that is a man's job, and you—"

"Are just as good with a gun as most men, and cooler headed to boot," she interjected.

"She has you there," Kane said from behind Donovan. Lillian smiled. Oh, she did like the man. He smiled back, his eyes dancing.

Donovan turned on his friend. "Weren't you leaving?"

"No, where would I go?"

"A bath wouldn't hurt," Donovan said and sneered.

"Why? She's seen me dirty, and I think she still likes me better than you," Kane said with a twinkle in his eye. "Isn't that right, love?"

"Well, you certainly are a lot nicer."

"See? She thinks I'm nicer." Kane chuckled and pounded his friend on the back. "Brother, you've got a lot to learn when it comes to women."

"Aren't you glad your sister didn't have him?" Lillian asked.

"Come to think of it—"

"Mac—"

"Okay, I'm leaving."

"It's about time," Donovan muttered.

"Is there some kind of trouble here?" Bruce walked up behind Kane. "Miss Lilly, do you need me to get rid of this guy?"

"Holy Moses," Kane muttered at the sight of the giant man.

"It's all right, Bruce," Lillian said. "This man is Kane Mc-Cormick. He's an old friend of Donovan's."

"Is that right? How come I've never seen you around here either?"

"I came up here to work at the Colbert mine after I discovered the piece I'd bought was salted."

"Salted?"

"Yeah." His fine fingers played with the brim of his coal-dusted hat. "Not more than a few ounces of silver at that. So I closed up the empty pit and took on where I'd actually get paid."

Bruce looked at Lillian.

"He's new in town," she said.

"You sure he's on the up-and-up?" Bruce crossed his arms over his chest.

"I'm as sure of him as I am of Donovan."

"Mac's coming back to take Lillian's place in the back room tonight," Donovan said. "She doesn't need to be bunked down here when she can be safely nursing her hurt ankle upstairs, don't you think?"

"I think whatever Miss Lilly wants," Bruce's deep voice rumbled. "That's my job."

The other two men looked at Lillian with astonishment. She raised an eyebrow at them. "What? Bruce is a good friend. You'll notice he's not ordering me about like I'm a silly-headed fluff."

"Miss Lilly is smarter than any other person I know," Bruce said. "I trust her a heck of a lot more than I trust you." He poked Donovan in the chest and sent Kane a narrow-eyed look. "Are you sure you don't want me to throw the both of them out?"

"I'm afraid the sheriff would get involved if you did that," Lillian said with a sigh. "They have laws about husbands and ownership."

"I could see my way into helping with that," Bruce said, tongue thoroughly planted in cheek. He was a big guy, but he was also smart as a whip and loved to tease. "Widow Lilly isn't a bad title."

Lillian saw Donovan's hands ball into fists and figured the teasing had gone far enough. "It's okay, Bruce. Right now I'm fine with being Mrs. West."

"Well, you let me know the second that changes," Bruce said.

"I will." Donovan sent her a withering look, and she simply blinked at him. It was time he knew that he couldn't just step in, take over, and expect her to be without some means of protecting herself. She wasn't that stupid.

"Okay, I'm off to the baths." Kane pounded Donovan on the back. "Try to stay alive at least until I get back." He took Lillian's hand and kissed the top of it. "Your beauty and intelligence are worthy of a queen. Let me know if you get tired of a quick draw. I'll be happy to show you how interesting slow can be."

Lillian thought she heard Donovan mutter something dark, but Donovan's face revealed nothing. The three men made their way across the store and stepped out, leaving the sound of the jangling bells and silence. She leaned forward and strained to hear what they said to each other outside, but they were too far away, and Donovan came back in before she could get up.

"I gave Bruce some money and asked him to take Mac out for supper. They'll bring us back something later."

"Oh, all right." Lillian settled back in her chair.

Donovan stalked his way across the floor and leaned down over her, his hands resting on her chair's armrests. She tilted back to keep distance between them.

"What?" she whispered.

"No more talk of being a widow," he said. "You can't be a widow until you know what it is to be a wife."

Her heart pounded at how near he was. At how much she wanted to kiss him. "And I don't know what that is?"

"Not yet." His words were a promise that got her heart rate up. Then he dipped his head and claimed her mouth with his own.

It was the first time he'd kissed her in days. The kiss was fierce, bold, and claiming with the promise of all kinds of things. It made her blood dance through her veins, and she clenched her hands to keep from grabbing him by the shirtfront and pulling him down on top of her.

He took her breath. He took her heart and maybe even a piece of her soul. Then he straightened and studied her. She couldn't help but note that his breath was coming about as fast as hers. Perhaps she had the same effect on him that he had on her.

"Soon," he promised, and then very gently tucked a stray strand of hair behind her ear. "Very soon, love."

"Promises, promises," she shot back.

This time he raised an eyebrow at her. His blue eyes captured her gaze, and she couldn't look away. The effect was like flying on the back of a horse racing toward the unknown, both exhilarating and terrifying.

He bent down and kissed her again, this one devastatingly short. "Oh, yeah, you can take that promise to the bank."

His hand cupped her jaw. His thumb brushed the side of her neck, and she closed her eyes and reveled in the wonder of his touch.

"I don't believe in banks," she said softly. "They are too easily robbed."

"Then believe in me," he said. "Because I believe in you."

She opened her eyes, and he was gone. Before she could stand up and see if he went to the back room, a customer came in and asked her about the price of a can of peaches.

She had to forget the mystery of the man who claimed to be her husband and concentrate on the livelihood she had built before the man had ever existed.

From where Donovan sat with his chair back leaning against the back of the store building, he could see both the alley to the left of the building and the outhouses and buildings behind. The sounds of drunken men echoed between the buildings. Occasionally he'd hear a fight break out and random gunshots.

The rifle in his lap was fully loaded.

There was a lot to think about. He hadn't considered how rowdy the West could be when hardworking men came to town with pockets full of money. It was like Dodge City when the cowboys came into town; locking everything down was the best bet until the drunks passed out and their money was all spent. Most of the women in the town were married or had families to protect them when things got rough. Those who didn't usually ended up working in the saloons. It wasn't pretty, but it was a way to survive.

Donovan thought about the woman he'd carried upstairs. She'd protested the whole way. Not that he blamed her. If this were his business, he'd be damned if someone else besides him were going to sit watch on a night like tonight.

Still, the thought of her lying awake with rifles beside her got his blood up. There was spunky and then there was darned foolish. It eased his anger a bit to know that she had hired Bruce to guard the store early on. But not before someone had messed with it and no man had been here to mess back.

He wondered what the town had thought of that. And where was the sheriff, anyway?

There was a crunch of footsteps on gravel and Donovan eased the rifle up, his finger on the trigger. "Declare yourself."

"It's me." Mac came around the corner holding a linen sack in one hand. "I brought you and Lillian some dinner."

Donovan relaxed back into his chair. "Thanks."

Mac went in the back door and reemerged with a second chair and rifle. He turned the chair so the back faced out and sat down. Silence settled around them, and Donovan could hear his friend thinking.

"What?"

"You're in love with her."

Choosing to ignore his friend's insight, he played dumb. "Who?"

Mac rested his arms across the back of the chair. "She is something."

Donovan didn't like the tone of his voice. Mac was a ladies' man, and Donovan knew who would win in that kind of contest. He narrowed his eyes. "What do you mean by that?"

"Spunky, quick-witted. That mouth on her, those eyes. I'd be in love with her if you weren't."

Silence. It was the only way to handle this volatile conversation. He let it sit between them a while before changing the subject. "What are the crowds like?" Donovan scanned the shadows. Maybe if he changed the subject, he wouldn't have to worry about the bump that his heart made at the idea of Mac loving Lillian.

"Some drunks, some rowdies, but it's early." Mac casually lifted one shoulder. "Most of the good townsfolk have boarded up and are tucked in for the night."

"Like Dodge when the cowboys are in town."

"Saloons are doing a darn good business. Of course, the damage to the buildings will cancel out some of the profits. I think the sheriff has four deputies on duty, roaming the streets in pairs."

Donovan sucked on his teeth thoughtfully. "What's that Bruce like?"

"Seems all right, pretty smart, as a matter of fact," Mac said. "He knew who you were. He was funning with you." Mac paused, and then continued. "He's in love with Lillian. So I'd watch your back if I were you. I think he was half-serious about making her a widow."

Donovan spit on the ground. "He can try."

"It's like that then." Mac grinned.

"Lot of good it does either of us, considering I'm not a storekeeper."

"Or her husband," McCormick pointed out. Donovan ground his teeth. The ruse was getting him in more trouble every day, and they had little to show for it.

"What's the word in the mines? Anyone touting easy money?"

"I've gotten wind of a place that's paying twice the going rate for an ounce of silver." Mac kept his eyes on the shadows.

"Where?"

"I don't know that yet. I'm still too new. The men don't trust me enough to let me in on the deal. Give me another week, and I'll be exchanging silver for counterfeit. How about on your end? Any leads?"

"Most of the townsfolk are on the up-and-up. They run a tab and then pay in silver at month's end. So far nothing counterfeit, but then I haven't taken a good look at today's cashbox. If you're right, then some of that counterfeit cash had to come in today with the miners looking for supplies."

"Bartenders and saloon owners are the ones who will lose out."

"Remind me next time to try that instead."

"Why? Bored with storekeeping?"

Donovan frowned. He wasn't, and that was something he wasn't ready to think about yet. "This whole mission is taking too much time. St. George is going to want some sort of report."

"Yeah, I know. I'll run over to Leadville and send out a telegram."

"Be careful. I don't want to draw any suspicion."

"What about Lillian?" Mac stared out.

"What about her?"

"She's smart. She has to have suspicions."

"I can handle her." Donovan leaned back in his chair.

Mac laughed. The sound of it danced around the darkening alley. "I wouldn't be surprised if she was the one handling you."

Donovan had to laugh too. "Well, now, better men than me have been handled by lesser women." He shook his head. "It's going to be interesting to see which one wins."

Chapter Ten

The next day, Donovan sifted through the cashbox. Sure enough there was a counterfeit bill. He held it up to the light and studied it. The ink was high quality and so was the engraving. If he weren't a trained expert there would be little chance he'd figure out that the bill wasn't real.

Glancing around to ensure he was alone, he slipped it into his pocket. Then he replaced it with a real one. He didn't want Lillian to become suspicious. She was very careful with her money, methodically matched each penny to the ledger.

He never asked her how much money she averaged in profit. But then again, she did her banking at the local establishment. All he had to do was go in and find out from Sandler how much was in their account.

Their account. It was a lie of course; it was Lillian's account. He had no right to it, and he knew it. That was a line he wouldn't cross. It was bad enough he'd taken over her life, lived in her home, pretended to own her business. He refused to go any deeper into her finances, no matter how bad he wanted to.

"What are you doing?"

Donovan looked up to see Lillian hobbling toward him. She had gotten quite good with the cane, and he suspected that by the end of the week she'd be back to 100 percent. Then his ability to keep ordering her about would go up in smoke. "I'm checking the cashbox against the receipts."

"And?"

"And it's on the nose." He closed the box. "You can double-check me if you want."

"I will," she said. "But first I wanted to let you know that we need to go to the Founders Day dance on Saturday."

"The Founders Day dance?"

"Yes," she said. "June first is the annual dance. It is very good for business and if you're going to still be here, then we had better go."

"I'll be here."

"All right," she said, unfazed. "Can you dance?"

"I've been known to escort a few ladies around the floor."

She took a deep breath and nodded. "Good. It's settled then."

He lifted the corner of his mouth. "Why, Miss Lillian, are you courtin' me?"

"What?" She scrunched her eyebrows together.

"Are you courting me?" A lovely shade of rose rushed up her neck and into her cheeks.

"I just thought . . ."

"What?" He put his elbow on the counter and rested his chin on his fist.

"Since you are telling everyone we're married—"

"We are married."

"Then we should go to the dance." She picked up the ledger. "That's what married people do."

"What do married people do?" He poked at her.

"Married people go to dances." Her tone was tinged with frustration. She leaned down to get the cashbox, and they were practically nose to nose. He liked the fact that she had a splash of freckles across the bridge of her nose. That her blue eyes had dark flecks in them. That her eyelashes were so pale you could barely see them. "Married people also kiss." She looked him in the eye, her tone a husky whisper. "Daily . . . sometimes hourly."

"Is that right?"

"Yes." The word came out in a dared whisper.

"And you know this how?"

"By watching all the other married people in town." Her gaze stuck on his mouth. All kinds of ideas came swimming into his head, and he found he liked them.

"We kissed," he pointed out.

"Not for a long time." She looked into his eyes, and he saw her innocent frustration.

"Come to think of it, it has been a while."

"Days." She sounded starved.

"I didn't want to take advantage of you." He wasn't sure if that was a lie or the truth.

"I don't believe that." She seemed to give up on the idea of getting him to kiss her and straightened. "Why, you've been taking advantage of me since you came to town."

"Not full advantage," he replied. A stab of guilt had gone through him. She was right; he had used her for no other reason than because he wanted to. What did she gain?

She froze for a second and then leaned in closer until they were a breath apart. "Why is that, Donovan West?" Her breath was sweet like mint against his lips. "Why haven't you taken full advantage?"

"I have no idea." He leaned forward to kiss her.

She straightened fast and hugged the cashbox. "Maybe you'd better start getting some ideas." Turning, she limped toward the door.

Donovan stood. "You wouldn't like the ideas I'm having," he warned her, his blood pumping.

"Now there, I think you're wrong." She looked at him over her shoulder. "I'm not fragile, Donovan. I'm a woman."

Women were more fragile than they ever imagined, Donovan thought as he watched her walk to the back room. He knew from experience.

He sat back down and drummed his fingers on the counter. Kissing led to sex and sex led to babies and women died in childbirth. End of story. He'd seen that firsthand. He didn't care if it happened to other people. What he cared about was it never happening again to a woman he loved.

Darn it, he'd done enough to Lillian by taking over like he did. He'd never be able to live with himself if he caused her any more harm.

He grabbed his hat and walked out the front door of the store. Time to get to work on the reason he was in Silverton. The sooner they cracked the case, the sooner he'd be back in Washington, D.C., and Lillian could go back to her life as an abandoned bride.

Lillian heard the doorbells jangle as he went out. She put the tea kettle on top of the small stove that served as both heat source and cooking surface for the back room. She lit the burner and bit her bottom lip.

He'd wanted to kiss her. In fact, if she hadn't pulled back, they would be kissing now. The thought had her toes curling in her shoes. Her hands trembled as she gathered a cup and saucer for her tea.

Silly, but she had to know. She had to know if he was even attracted to her. He acted like it, but he never did anything about it. Why?

She sat down and felt the heat of embarrassment rush back over her cheeks. He'd said she was courting him. Was she? As far as she knew, courting was how a man and a woman figured out if they liked each other well enough to get married.

Seems Donovan, if that was his real name, had skipped that step.

Did she want that? Lillian had always thought of herself as a practical woman. Why would she want romance from a man she was already shackled to?

It wasn't romance she wanted. It was the truth.

Clearly Donovan wasn't immune to her kisses. There were five days until the dance. Five days to work Donovan up into such a frenzy, he'd tell her anything. Once he did, she'd have to give in, of course, and do a whole lot more than kissing.

The thought of giving in had her heart banging against her ribs and her palms breaking out in a sweat. It was a win-win situation. She'd give in and find out not only why he was in town, but also what the benefits were of having a man around. So far, there weren't many.

Clearly there was something more, and she was bound and determined to find out what.

*   *   *

Donovan spotted Bart Johnson leaving the feed store. He was their main suspect. Donovan's boss, St. George, had received a tip that Johnson was known to associate with the counterfeiters. In fact, Donovan and McCormick had followed him out to Silverton. But following Johnson had been a big fat waste of time, so he'd come up with this new plan in hopes of catching whoever else might be involved. However, Johnson's suspicions about Donovan complicated things.

Donovan rubbed the counterfeit bill he'd shoved into his pocket and headed toward the feed store. Maybe he'd have a chat with Art Williams, the owner. See if he had gotten any odd bills lately.

It was a gamble, alerting the other businessmen that there might be phony money running through town, but it was time the pot got stirred up just a bit. If people knew what they were looking for, it would squeeze the gang a little. Maybe even enough for them to show their hand.

The worst that would happen was for the ring to pick up and move on to another area. Not the best outcome, but then again maybe it was best for Lillian's sake.

He walked into the feed store. "Hey, Jake." He nodded to one of the two men playing cards in the back corner. "Harold."

"Donovan," Jake replied. "What brings you to the feed store?" He rocked on the back two legs of his chair and squinted at his cards.

"I'm looking for Art. Is he around?"

"He's out loading Old Man Jackson's wagon."

"Thanks." Donovan walked through the room and out the back door. Unlike the general store, the feed store was more of a hangout for the local men. Women had no reason to buy feed. The fifty-pound bags tended to keep them away.

Donovan had taken to hiding out here whenever things with Lillian got a bit too hot. It gave him an excuse to get to know the men in town, blend in.

He found Art and his son, Pete, tossing immense bags of feed into a wagon. Donovan leaned against the wagon and watched.

"Hey, Mr. West," Pete said. "How are you?"

"Fine, fine." Donovan turned to the old man. "Art, how's business?"

"Good enough." Art tossed the last bag into the wagon. He eyed Donovan. "Not good enough for you to get into."

Donovan laughed. "I'm not looking to sell feed," he said. "I've got my hands full with what I've got now."

"I'd say," Art said. "That little lady of yours is more than a handful."

"Is she going to the dance?" Pete asked. Donovan noted the twin spots of red in the young man's cheeks.

"We're going," Donovan drawled the words out.

"Mind if I ask her to dance?" Pete swallowed hard. "I mean, there aren't too many girls . . . I mean ladies to practice . . . I mean . . ."

"She's a married woman." Donovan sent the kid a look.

"Oh, no." He raised his hands. "I just would like to dance."

"Then we'll see what she says come Saturday."

"Thanks." The kid grinned. He shoved his hands into his pockets and backed off. "Thanks."

Art watched him leave and shook his head. "You were gone for so long, the single men started thinking maybe she was a widow." He turned his steely gaze on Donovan. "A man should never leave his young wife that long. Commission or not."

"Trust me, the only way I'll leave her again is if she's a widow," Donovan said. He meant it. When the case was over, he'd always planned to kill off Donovan West and give Lillian some legitimacy in town.

"So what sent you out this way?" Art slapped his hand onto Donovan's shoulder. The two men walked back into the store. "Isn't it about suppertime?"

"I thought I'd stop in before I go to the café and pick up something."

"You'd be better off spending the money having Mrs. Sanchez teach your wife to cook."

"Maybe so," Donovan said. "But I'd rather not starve."

The men laughed. "Oh, come on now," Art said. "Half the fun of being a newlywed is putting up with your wife learning to cook. I remember when my Judy first tried to make pot roast and biscuits. The meat was tough as nails and burned on the bottom. The biscuits benefited from dipping in the runny gravy. We still laugh about it now."

"Yes, well, Lillian makes a good pie." Donovan remembered the apple pie that had ended up on his shirt and what followed. He shoved his hands into his pockets when the zing of desire rushed through him.

Art laughed and pushed a chair Donovan's way. "Sit down and take a load off." He reached behind the seed tin and pulled out a whiskey bottle, opened it up, took a swig, and handed it to Donovan.

Donovan took a long pull and sighed when the heat of the whiskey hit the back of his throat. Nope, married townsmen didn't go to the saloon. They had their own stashes well hidden from the wives. Even the preacher pretended to look the other way.

"Listen, I was wondering if you ever had anyone try to pass you a phony treasury bill." Donovan handed Art the bottle back.

Art narrowed his eyes and frowned. "Not that I know of. There's a lot of strangers come through, so I keep an eye out for that kind of thing. Why?"

"I pulled this out of the weekend's till." Donovan took the bill out of his pocket and handed it to Art. "I had me a run-in with counterfeiters back East, so I know a thing or two about it. Take a look at this, and tell me what you think."

"Hmm," the old man said and held it up. He walked over to the window and pressed it against the glass. "Looks good. I wouldn't be suspicious at all if it wasn't so crisp." He snapped the bill and handed it back to Donovan. "We don't git too many crisp bills out this way."

"That's what I thought," Donovan said. "Then I got to really looking at it. See this here?"

"That blob under the eagle?"

"Yeah, that should be a signature."

"Huh, you're right." Art took the bill. "I swear it looks like two wavy lines. Something with a B and an S. B.S. It's like the forger is making fun of us."

"Do you think you've gotten any of these?"

Art pulled his bills out of his pocket. "All I've got on me is what I made today." He thumbed through the bills. "Nope, nothing, but then I wouldn't expect anything today. Just had a few regulars in after the miners left this morning."

Donovan tipped his chair back. "I saw Bart Johnson."

"Yeah, he stopped by and ordered some feed for his horses. Said he'd be by to pick it up this weekend."

When all the miners were in town, passing counterfeit bills would be easier, Donovan thought. He kept that to himself. "Probably wouldn't hurt to cash in the paper for gold."

"To do that you'd have to go into Denver. The mint there will do the cashing," Art said and spit. "Good thing most pay in silver coin around here."

"Silver's a handful to carry," Donovan commented. "Paper money is easier to handle."

"Sounds to me like you were part of the paper party."

"I agreed with them, if that's what you mean." Donovan leaned the chair back against the wall. "Most people did, I figure, or the banks would have had a run on gold."

"Heard tell the federal government has enough gold to cover paper." Art took another swig of whiskey.

"I heard that too, but I don't see anyone caring to trade theirs in."

Art offered Donovan the bottle, but he waved it away. "Maybe you should," Art said sagely. "Seeing as how that piece you've got is phony."

"Maybe I'll make a new policy of silver or gold only."

"Huh, might be wise," Art said thoughtfully. "Wonder how Fred Sandler at the bank will take that."

"Why?"

"Well, now." Art spit into a nearby spittoon. "All us businessmen going to silver an' gold might cramp the banker's style a bit."

"Why? Does he exchange a lot of silver for paper?"

"Naw, but he does a lot of business with the mining companies. They like to pay out in paper, keep the silver to themselves. Claim it's easier for them to haul it out to the mints. You know what I mean?"

"Sandler provides the dollars for the companies and in turn they pass them on to the miners."

"Yeah, not so sweet a deal if the local businesses won't take the paper money for goods."

So by warning the locals about the counterfeit ring, he just might be stepping into a sweet deal between the banker and the mining companies. Maybe even into the heart of the counterfeit ring. Now that would be something.

Donovan got up and shook Art's hand. "Guess I'd better go if I hope to have something good to take home for supper."

"Thanks for the info on the counterfeit. Think I'll put up a sign before Friday," Art said. "Maybe even have a talk with the other business owners. See if anyone else was passed anything suspicious."

"Not a problem," Donovan said. "Wanted to see if I was the only sucker in town."

"Hopefully so." Art smacked Donovan's back. "Could be someone was just funning with you, seeing as how you're new an' all."

"Could be," Donovan said. "Not unusual to pull a fast one on the new guy."

"Not unusual at all." Art closed the door behind Donovan.

Donovan stepped out into the street and eyed the people milling about. Bart Johnson was nowhere to be seen. Probably in the saloon. Donovan turned in the opposite direction. He'd accomplished what he'd set out to do. That was to warn the other business owners. If Bart were part of the ring, word would get out come Saturday that their funny money wasn't welcome here.

Nothing like stirring a hornet's nest to find out how many insects hid inside.

Chapter Eleven

It was darned hard to seduce information out of a man who wasn't around. Lillian used the feather duster on the stack of canned goods. Just three weeks ago, she'd have been content to dust the shop alone on such a lovely summer morning.

She glanced out the windows to see that the sky was bright blue. The outside temperature was nice enough that she had the windows open, and a sweet mountain breeze fluttered her lace curtains.

The tearoom across the street opened for lunch. A wagon full of milled two-by-fours bounced past the windows. It was the Wednesday before Founders Day, and the mayor had two young boys from the school climbing on street poles and putting up red, white, and blue bunting. Mrs. Mayor stood off to the side and shouted out directions.

Lillian ran the duster along the windowsill and kept an eye on the streets. Where was Donovan? Why had he been so impossible to pin down? It was as if he knew she planned on seducing him.

She sighed. Seduction was not one of her skills. The near kiss had sent him running. When he'd come back, they'd shared dinner, but then he'd gone downstairs and sat in the back room writing something in a book.

When she'd asked, he hadn't even looked up. All he'd said was that it was plans for a possible expansion of the store. Her store. She opened her mouth to argue, but he'd turned his back on her.

Fine, she'd thought. Then she'd gone back upstairs and eaten by herself, just like she always had. Let him plot whatever in his notebook; it gave her time to plot her seduction upstairs.

"Morning, Lillian," Mildred, the mayor's wife, called through the open window. "I saw your husband this morning. So glad to see him around. Is he home for good now?"

"Unless the army needs him, he's here for good," Lillian said. It was the lie she had heard Donovan tell the townspeople and a lie that made sense.

"Then is he looking to start mining? Maybe buy a stake?"

"We haven't talked about it. Why?" Lillian asked.

"Hmm, well, I saw him talking to one of the miners this morning. Then they rode off together. So perhaps he has decided without you." The mayor's wife tilted her head knowingly. Her eyes glittered with curiosity.

"Perhaps he has." Lillian didn't give in to her urge to close the window on the nosy woman. "I'm sure I'll find out tonight when he gets home."

"I'm sure you will." The old woman turned her attention back to her husband and the boys draping bunting. "No, no, you dolts, not like that. Hang it so it drapes." She waved her hand in a swoop to emphasize her point and walked off.

Lillian took a deep breath and turned back to her dusting. She wondered if it had been Kane McCormick that Donovan had met that morning. What was McCormick's connection to the man who pretended to be her husband? Why had Donovan been even more standoffish since the mysterious Mr. McCormick had appeared?

Were they working together? If so, what con were they up to, and why did they pick her? Clearly, if it was her money he wanted, Donovan would have already sold her shop and left her high and dry. Instead, he hung around Silverton, pretending to be her husband and getting to know the townspeople. Why?

The doorbells jangled. "Well now, Mrs. West, how are you?"

She met Art Miller at the front of the store. "I'm good, and yourself, Mr. Miller?"

"Not too bad. Say, nice display." He nodded toward the hats she had set up in the window.

"Thank you."

"I need a chaw of tobacco please."

"Certainly." She pulled a tin of chewing tobacco from behind the counter and rang it up. "That comes to fifteen cents."

"Got it." He pulled the coins out of his pocket and handed them to her. "So, make any more apple pies lately?" he asked and winked.

Lillian frowned. "What?"

"Ah, Donovan told me all about how good you were at apple pie," Art said with a sly smile. "You know the old saying."

Lillian's heart flipped. She felt heat rush to her cheeks at the ribbing. "Which saying is that?"

"The way to a man's heart is through his stomach." He winked again.

What had Donovan said? "Is Donovan complaining about my cooking?" she asked, confused.

"Oh, no, ma'am. He was just complimenting you on your pie making." Art took his tin and tipped his hat her way. "Good day now, Mrs. West. Oh, and thank Donovan for the tip on paper."

"Okay, I will." Lillian was seriously confused. First off, what apple pie was Art talking about? Second, the way to a man's heart? Oh! Lillian felt the heat rise to her cheeks. She pressed them with her palms.

Had Donovan told Art about how she had kissed him and then smashed a pie between them? Embarrassment was followed by anger. What was he doing kissing and telling?

The way to a man's heart was through his stomach. Humph. She picked up her duster and furiously cleaned the shelves of goods. She wasn't a cook. She'd never been a cook. Pie making was something she did for fun. If he was complaining . . .

She stopped. Maybe he wasn't complaining. Art had made it sound like a compliment. Maybe he hinted that she should be kissing her husband more.

Well! She would be if the man stuck around like he told her he would.

"Maybe he'd stick around if you cooked more often," she

muttered to the air. Her mind played with the possibilities. Perhaps feminine wiles weren't the only way to get a man's attention. She remembered how the men's heads all turned when Mrs. Sanchez had pies cooling on the windowsill.

Lillian decided she would make a pie that very night. Maybe the pie would get his attention long enough for him to answer some of her questions.

Donovan got back into town later than he'd hoped to. He settled his horse in the small stable behind the store. It was nearly midnight by the town hall clock. He wondered if Lillian had left the door unlocked for him or if he was going to have to break in.

He and Mac had spent the day going over the local terrain, looking for anything that might serve as a printing area. But there were hundreds of abandoned mines in the mountains, a few dozen shacks, and nothing suspicious. They had called it quits when the sun went down over the top of the mountains.

The back of the building was uninviting. The rear windows had bars over them to curb the weekend rowdiness. The porch light was out, and the door appeared highly unfriendly. He tried the handle. It was locked.

Donovan frowned. He pounded on the door, but there was no answer. The last thing he wanted to do was alert the neighbors. Looking around, he spied a rain barrel and figured it was half as tall as the back porch roof.

There was no point of entry from the back. Only the downstairs room had windows. The upper part of the house held the kitchen and a pantry. Neither one had windows. That luxury was left for the false front.

There was nothing to do now but go for it. He rolled up his sleeves and grabbed hold of the pillar. He climbed onto the rim of the barrel and hoisted himself up onto the porch roof.

He gauged the height of the roof from where he stood. Then he jumped up and grabbed hold of the gable and pulled himself up and over. He rested on the roof for a few minutes, catching his breath. The stars twinkled down at him, as if to poke fun of the fact that he had been locked out of his own home.

Would she have locked him out if it were really his home? Then another thought made him frown. If it was this easy for him to get inside, how easy was it for anyone else?

He rolled to his feet and walked across the roof to the false front. The light from her window shone down onto the street. Listening carefully, he didn't hear any movement inside. It took but a moment for him to ease over the side and land with a soft thud on the balcony.

Maybe she wanted him to come in her window. After all, it was the only room lit. Maybe he'd avoid the temptation. Donovan moved to the dark parlor window. He eased the window open and slid one leg over into the shadowy interior.

The click of a shotgun being cocked sounded through the silence and froze him in his tracks. "Lillian?"

"Move one muscle, and I'll fill your backside with pellets."

"It's me, Donovan." His heart was in his ears, and he hoped she didn't shoot.

"Who?"

Now that was just plain mean. "Your husband, Donovan West," he said. "Now put down the gun and let me in before the neighbors start talking."

"The neighbors are already talking." There was a scratch and the flare of a match illuminated her face. She looked mad. Donovan wondered at the folly of leaving her alone all day and then coming in through the window. Now that he thought about it, he should have spent the night in the stable.

"Can I come in?" he asked, ignoring the cold sweat that trickled down his back.

"Fine, but throw your gun down first."

He noted that she didn't take her finger off the trigger as he untied his gunbelt and tossed it on the floor. Donovan stepped in and held his hands in the air. She picked up his gun, tucked it beside her, and put the rifle in her lap. She lit the wick on the hurricane lamp, trimmed it, and then put the glass cover over it. Her eyes glittered when she turned her attention back to him. It made his mouth go dry. "What kind of man comes home late and sneaks in an upstairs window?"

"The kind who doesn't have a key to his own home."

"Maybe we should talk about that, since as you can see I found my rifle and it's loaded." She slid her hand up and down the rifle.

"Okay." He was going to take this one slow. "But don't you think it would be suspicious if you shot me?"

"Don't worry, the buckshot won't kill you." She looked up at him, her expression solemn as a poker player.

Good God, she was gorgeous when she was angry. He couldn't help his grin or his step forward. Of course, he stopped dead in his tracks when her finger made the first click on the trigger.

"Now, darling," he said.

"Don't you 'darling' me." She narrowed her eyes. "You've been manipulating me for weeks, had me at your mercy. Playing with my store, my life, my tender feelings."

"Your tender feelings?"

She shook her head and rolled her eyes. "I don't know why, but I like you. I do. In fact, I planned on seducing you tonight."

"Seducing me?" His mouth went dry.

She kept her gaze steady. "Until you didn't come home. At first I was worried. I mean, my husband was not where he should be. Then . . . then I remembered you are not my husband. And if you were out carousing, I had no right to care."

"I wasn't out carousing, love. Really."

"It doesn't matter, because, you see, I found my gun and you . . . well, you were crawling in my window after midnight. I think no one would argue that you deserved to be shot."

"Now, darling, we both know if you were going to shoot me you would have done it already." A nervous twinge cramped his stomach. Here was the woman he'd seen take down Bart Johnson.

"Oh, I planned on shooting you the minute you came through the window, but then I got to thinking that I should ask you some questions while I had the upper hand." Her expression was calm and a bit scary. "I think it's time you tell me who you really are and why you're pretending to be Donovan West."

"Is this just because you thought I was out with another woman?"

She reacted by bringing the gun up to her shoulder. Donovan took a step back and raised his hands, palms up. "Okay, all right, I'm sorry if I insulted you. I should know by now that you are far too intelligent to not see through my ruse."

"Go on."

"Truth is I'm working for the government," Donovan said. "I'm a Secret Service agent."

"Right, and I'm the First Lady."

"No, really." He eased his hand into his shirt pocket and pulled out his wallet. "My credentials." He flashed them at her.

The gun barrel lowered a notch. "Why are you in Silverton, and why are you pretending to be my husband?"

"Can I sit down?"

She pointed with the gun toward the settee. "All right."

He made himself comfortable on the couch and paused a moment to take in his surroundings. The room smelled of freshly baked pie and kerosene from the lamp. The light made a halo around her. Lillian wore her robe and nightgown. Her hair was down in a long fat braid that ran over her shoulder. Her pale skin gleamed like porcelain in the light.

She was a sight he'd never forget as long as he lived.

"Your name?"

"Let's just keep it Donovan West." He held up one hand when she lifted the gun. "Seriously. Everyone knows me as Donovan here; let's not change that. Trust me, you don't want the townsfolk to think you've been living in sin for the past few weeks."

"I haven't," she said.

He thought he detected disappointment in the statement. At least, he hoped. He shook off the thought.

"All right, Donovan. Why are you in Silverton, and why are you pretending to be my husband?"

"My partner and I were sent here to investigate reports of a counterfeit ring."

"Your partner . . . Kane McCormick?"

"Yes." He nodded. "I needed some way to blend into the community."

"How did you know?"

"That you made up a husband?" He shrugged. "I saw you take down Bart Johnson in the alley."

A sweet blush ran up her neck. He smiled. She was embarrassed. He would not have believed she could be embarrassed.

"He can be an awful pest."

"I overheard him saying that he didn't believe you were really married. That no one had ever seen your husband. So I did some checking."

Concern clouded her expression. "You did some checking?"

"Yes, it took me about a day to figure out that you'd conned the whole town into thinking you were married."

"It wasn't a con," she said. "It was, well, business. I'd tried it on my own, but no one wanted to do steady business with a single woman."

"Smart," he said, and she lowered the gun onto her lap. "Mind if I ask how you got the cash to get started?"

Something in her visibly relaxed, as if she had her answers and was about to give him his. "I worked as a maid and a seamstress for four years," she said. "But I wanted to be more, to have more." She got up and put the gun on the table. "Do you want some pie?"

"Sure." He stayed put, uncertain of her mood. "So you saved up the money and came out West to start your own business."

"Like I said, no one took me seriously." She took out two plates and forks. "I was in Leadville first. I had the banker there verify that I had more than enough money to rent a building and stock it. But the menfolk refused to have anything to do with a woman proprietor. The ladies all shook their skirts at me as if I were running a house of ill repute."

She cut the pie and placed it on a plate. "Tea?"

"I prefer coffee."

He watched her put the hot water on to boil. Then she brought him a plate and a fork. "One kind old woman asked me why I was so interested in having a store. Why didn't I just get married like a good girl?"

"That's when it occurred to you to pretend to be married?" He took the pie from her and watched her go back into the kitchen.

"I thought about actually getting hitched." She took down the coffee grinder. Tossing in a fistful of beans, she turned the handle. The crunching sound told him that the beans were being ground and filling the air with the smell of fresh coffee.

He liked the way she wiggled as she churned. It was a homey sight, this lovely woman, standing in her robe, barefoot and making him coffee. For a moment he wished it would last forever.

"Why didn't you?" he asked. "Get married."

She glanced over her shoulder. "There wasn't much to choose from, being as most of the men were grubbing stakes. And the store owners all had wives." She poured the grounds into a coffee press and poured in the boiling water. "It's not like a woman can bring in a mail-order husband." She pulled two mugs out of the cupboard and put them on the counter. Then she pressed the grounds down and poured the coffee into the mugs.

The smell wafted toward him and permeated the room, as tempting as the pie on the plate he held. He was a Southern gentleman and waited for her to sit down and join him.

"Besides, I checked the laws. If I got married, my husband could take all the money I worked so hard for and do whatever he wanted with it." She brought him his mug and set it down on the table beside the settee. "I've seen too many good women give all their hard-earned cash to a man in the name of love."

"So you decided to make up a husband."

She laughed. It was short and leaned toward self-deprecating. "Donovan West," she said and waved toward him. "He was the perfect match. Let me spend the money wisely while he spent his days being an American hero."

He watched her sit down with just the cup of coffee between her hands. She left her pie on the counter.

"You can go ahead and eat that," she said.

"What about yours?"

"I've decided that I'm not in the mood."

Donovan was starved, and the pie smelled good. A man didn't need a second invitation. He dug his fork into the crisp crust and took a bite. First there was the crunchy pastry top, followed by the sweet strawberry taste, chased by tart rhubarb. He closed his eyes. "I've died and gone to heaven."

"Thank you," she said. "I made the pie for you."

"You did?" He felt surprise and then pleasure fill him.

"Yes. Art walked by and mentioned to me that you said you liked my apple pie."

"I did."

She studied him over the top of her coffee cup. "You didn't get to eat the pie."

"I tasted enough of it to know that I enjoyed it." He put his plate down. "A lot." He leaned forward and looked her square in the eye.

"What are we going to do now?" Lillian sipped her coffee and tried to ignore the meaning in his look.

"I think that all depends on what you want to do, Miss Lillian."

Chapter Twelve

Oh, boy, Lillian should be thrilled. The minute he'd climbed through her window the world had righted itself. She had her gun and was back in control of her life. So why was she a tangle of emotion? Had some part of her actually thought . . . secretly hoped . . . he might want to make this marriage real?

She clutched the smooth coffee mug and didn't take her eyes off Donovan's handsome face.

"So, you're a Secret Service agent pretending to be my husband, whom we both know I invented."

"Yes."

He had told the truth. He was a good guy, not a bad guy out for her money. At least that was something. "You're using my story as a cover to investigate a ring of counterfeiters in the area."

"Right again." His gaze drew her, and she felt the fine tremble start in her hands.

Donovan got up, dusted off his hands, and stalked forward. She leaned back in her chair. Her heart rate picked up. For goodness' sake, the man was gorgeous. He had on a blue denim shirt and tan pants. The sleeves of the shirt were rolled up, revealing strong forearms and square hands. Hands that had touched her before and made her skin tingle.

His boots knocked at her floor as he came toward her.

"We're not married," she said, more to remind herself than him.

"Nope, we're not." He stood over her.

"We're just pretending."

124

"That's right." He took the mug out of her numb fingers and raised her chin by tugging it gently up. Then he leaned down so that his lips were a mere heartbeat away.

His breath smelled sweet, like strawberry pie, tangy rhubarb, and coffee. Her whole body was on alert.

"Tell me something, Donovan." Her voice was barely a whisper over the beating of her heart. "Are you a man of action?"

"Yes." To prove his point, he leaned down and kissed her. It was more of a claiming than a kiss.

She clutched his shoulders. The world swung as he kissed her, light as a feather and more precious than gold. It touched her soul and changed her somehow.

Lillian had no idea she kept her feelings so locked up and protected against the world. It must have been a talent learned in the orphanage. It was a talent he dismissed with one kiss.

"Now what?" she whispered.

"Now I do what I should have done from the beginning."

"And that is?"

"Ask for your help, Lillian."

"What?"

He paced in front of her. "I know I have no right, but I'm going to ask you to help me and Mac catch our counterfeiters." He had his hands behind his back and stopped. "There was a counterfeit bill in the cashbox."

"Seriously?"

"Seriously." His mouth made a grim line. "There will be more where that came from if we don't catch this ring. So, Lillian, will you help us?"

She swallowed and bit her bottom lip. "What do I need to do?"

Donovan stared up at the tin ceiling and watched it lighten as the sun came up. His heart was heavy. Lillian had taken the truth very well. She had even agreed to allow him to continue his ruse, had even promised to give him a key to the store, and she had asked for nothing in return.

That was the part that got him. If she were a real con she would have demanded something in exchange, but she didn't. Instead, she looked at him with an emotion in her eye that his heart was not ready for. An emotion that said she liked having him around a bit too much.

But he didn't make any promises. Instead, he continued to use her, bunking on her parlor floor, keeping up the ruse. In the end he'd solve his case and go home. She would be the one left to deal with the emotion in her eyes.

Someone ought to kick him in the backside for that.

She deserved to be married. She deserved a husband who would always be there for her, protect her. She deserved better than this pretense.

Donovan swore under his breath. It didn't matter what he felt. He would never marry again. What if she got pregnant? What if he killed another woman who carried his child? It didn't matter what anyone said; he knew in his heart he wouldn't ever go through that again.

Guilt got him out of the bed. Lillian was everything he'd ever dreamed of in a woman. He couldn't bring himself to think about how he'd treated her.

He got dressed. The dawning light showed him the remains of coffee and pie. The window curtains fluttered from the wind that blew in through the still-open window.

He had some hard thinking to do, and here was not the place to do it. He threw his stuff together and rolled up the bundle he'd been sleeping on for the past three weeks. Socks stuffed into boots, he took one last look back.

It was clear he couldn't stay here and hurt her further. Something had to be done to protect her from him. He'd bunk with Mac from now on and sneak into the store before anyone else was the wiser. That way he could keep up the ruse without doing further damage to Lillian.

Knowing Lillian, she'd be mad as hell. Better mad than broken. He'd have a talk with her about how it was better for her if he put some distance between them.

* * *

Lillian woke up to sunlight streaming into her window. Sitting up, she thought about everything Donovan had said the night before. It was hard to imagine a counterfeit ring in Silverton. But then again, the silver rush had brought all kinds of things to the Colorado mountains, good and bad. Lucky for her it had brought Donovan.

He wasn't a varmint or a scallywag. No, he was an agent of the federal government, and he was going to let her help. Pride nestled around her heart. She always did have a thing for a man with a gun and a badge.

She padded barefoot into the kitchen and lit the burner in her small coal stove. Then she poured water from the pitcher into her teapot, putting it on to heat. Coffee would be just the thing to wake her up and get her day started.

She looked about her parlor.

The window was open. The curtains fluttered in the soft mountain wind. The wind told her that it would be a warm day, bringing the dry scent of the street below and the flowers that blossomed purple on the mountainside.

But the window wasn't what bothered her. Nor was it the remains of last night's coffee and pie. She looked the parlor over again and it hit her what was wrong.

Donovan's things were gone.

In that second, her body turned cold. Her once glowingly warm skin ran gooseflesh over it. She shivered as if someone had walked over her grave.

His bunk blankets were gone. His mess kit with his shaving toiletries . . . all gone. She looked around for a note, some sort of explanation. There was nothing. Only the sound of the town waking up and the miners gathering for their morning travel up the mountain to the mines.

She glanced out the window. Everything looked normal. Paula opened the dress shop across the street. The Bruenheart boy swept the walk in front of the bank. A pair of horses and riders headed off down the street. People said their good mornings.

The sky was blue, the mountain bursting with spring color.

Everything was normal, except Donovan was gone. Had everything he'd said last night been a lie?

Something inside her froze up. She blinked dry eyes and let the curtains fall back. Her clock chimed eight. She needed to get dressed. She was going to be late opening the store today and people would wonder why.

Chapter Thirteen

Y ou're late coming down."

Lillian startled at the sound of Donovan's voice. She turned to find him sitting alone in the back room, watching her. "I thought you left."

"No, we had a plan, remember?" His voice was a low caress against her skin. She cautioned her heart not to make anything out of his words.

"Your stuff is gone."

"Yeah . . . about that." He stood up. "I'm moving in with McCormick for the remainder of my time here."

"All right." She hated the confusion inside her. Hated feeling like a foolish schoolgirl with an infatuation that was unrequited. "Why?"

"There is so much we should talk about." He tucked a stray hair behind her ear. "I can't talk to you up there."

"Why not?" she asked, confused. This whole thing was absurd. An emotional roller coaster, she clutched her hands in her apron and tried not to think about how she had assumed he had left her for good. That he had lied. Yet here he stood. She realized she didn't know him at all. How could she think she was falling in love?

"Truthfully," he said, "all I want to do is make love to you. If I stay down here in public view, then I have to keep my hands off you."

Lillian grew brave. "What if I don't want you to keep your hands off me?"

He blew out a breath at her words. His eyes grew dark, and he stepped closer. She let him. Her heart banged against her rib cage.

"Don't say things like that to me. And for God's sake, don't look at me like that," he said low, his voice practically a growl.

"Fine." She moved closer to the curtain and turned on him. "I don't understand. Why are you like this? What is it about me that makes you take a step forward and then two steps back? Because I'm confused and, frankly, hurt."

He shoved his hands into his pockets. "I was married once."

Lillian swallowed the words that threatened to spill out. Instead, she waited.

"Susan died two years ago."

"I'm sorry." Pity filled her, and Lillian took a step toward him. He raised his hand to stop her.

"Don't."

She froze. "Okay."

"Susan was the most beautiful woman I had ever seen." He paced the floor with his hands in his pockets. His words shredded Lillian's heart. She knew she wasn't a great beauty. She never had been, never would be. "All I wanted to do was protect her, care for her, keep her safe.

"Instead, I killed her." He stopped and looked at Lillian. There was such pain and despair in his eyes that her heart broke with the ache of it. She bit her lip and waited. "I should never have married her," he said. "She was so delicate, too delicate."

Lillian frowned. He'd killed her by marrying her? How the heck could you do that?

"We were going to have a son," he went on. This time his eyes held a far-off look as he slumped against the desk. "She was too weak to hold my child." His gaze locked with Lillian's. "Susan died. There was nothing I could do. I can still hear her cries."

"And the baby?" Lillian asked in a dry-mouthed whisper.

"Never took a breath."

She disciplined herself not to move. Not to go to him and hold him against this horror that still scarred his heart.

"My mother named him William, and we buried them together." He paused, his mouth a tight line. "I packed up, sold the farm, and began my work with the government."

"I see." Lillian waited for him to breathe again, for his skin to show some color. It would, after a while, when the aching memory slid and hid. She knew. She'd seen enough of it in her lifetime.

When his color returned, she stepped up in front of him. Her skirts brushed his legs, her hands behind her so that she would not touch him. Not yet. He was too vulnerable. "I'm not going to die," she said as gently as possible. "Trust me, I'm a sturdy gal. Little, but sturdy."

He looked at her with haunted eyes. "I should never have married her."

"I'm not her."

"Pregnancy kills."

"Some women," she agreed. "But not all. Or there wouldn't be so many women with five children hanging on their skirts."

"If I stayed with you . . ." His gaze went to her stomach. "If we—"

"It's what married people do." She touched his shoulder, but he brushed her aside and strode away from her.

"You will get pregnant." He shook his head. "I can't. I vowed on Susan's grave to never, ever let that happen again."

"That is simply unreasonable." She balled up her hands. "People live and die all the time. What is important is that you live when you get the chance."

"I made a vow." His chin grew stubborn.

"But you still liked my pie." She let a small smile flit around her mouth. He remained unmoved, and she felt frustration grow at his pigheadedness. "Fine, then. You go sleep with your friend. What will the neighbors think? Hmm? Did you think of that?"

"I could come and go early enough. They would—"

"Know the minute you moved out. This is a small town,

Donovan. You'll attract attention. People will talk and specu-
late and maybe even discover your secret . . . and mine. I won't
have it."

"I don't care what you will have or not," he said in a furious
whisper. "It's bad enough that I—"

"What? Used me? Yeah, now *that* I agree with. You could
have told me instead of stepping in and taking over my life
without so much as a how-do-you-do. But you did and now
you have to live with the consequences."

"You could have been involved with the ring." From the
tone of his voice, she knew that he knew it sounded stupid. "I
couldn't tell you."

"Well, here we are. You and your partner mixed up in my
life. I won't have the neighbors thinking I am somehow responsible for driving my husband away . . . again. Sleep here
in the back room if you can't bring yourself to come upstairs.
But don't go running off, at least not until you've finished your
job and are gone for good." She eyed him. "Just how were you
planning on explaining your disappearance when your little
assignment was over?"

"I planned on some excuse, probably get recalled into the
army." He crossed his arms over his chest. "Men do it all
the time. There is always some skirmish or other. Once I'm gone,
you can run things your way again."

"And that would be that."

"That's how it played in my head."

"I see." She bit her lip. "What if I don't want that? What if
I want you to stay?"

He looked at her and for one sad moment she thought she
saw horror in his eyes. That small flash of emotion pierced her
heart, leaving her numb.

"Don't worry," she said and gave him a light-hearted laugh.
"It's not likely I'll pitch a fit about your leaving. If you can't
tell already, I'm selfish. I don't play well with others. The last
thing I want is a man taking over my business and messing
with my affairs."

She turned on her heel. "I think I heard someone knocking."

She left him to the darkness of the back room, needing time alone. To think about everything that had been done. To figure out what she wanted and how she was going to get it.

"You told her?"

Donovan frowned and walked his horse along the winding mountain path. He kept his gaze on the terrain. "She had a shotgun to my groin."

"So you told her who we are and what is going on. How do you know she won't go blurting it to everyone in town?" Mac's concern was genuine.

"She won't," Donovan said, stubborn and grumpy from guilt and lack of sleep.

"How do you know?"

"I just know."

Mac stopped in his tracks. "Shoot, you slept with her."

Donovan shot his partner a nasty look. "I did not."

"You did. You slept with her. Unbelievable. The honorable, self-disciplined Donovan brought down by a feisty redhead."

"No . . . I . . . did . . . not." Lust, frustration, and heartbreak filled him at the thought of her.

"Good God, man, you told her we were Secret Service agents, and then you slept with her. This changes everything."

"It changes nothing," Donovan snapped. "Don't worry about Lillian. She's not part of the gang. She won't tell."

"So what happened this morning?"

"What do you mean what happened this morning?"

"You know, when she woke up after. Did she accuse you of debasement? Or did she have stars in her eyes. Man, if she had stars in her eyes, you are in some deep trouble."

Donovan felt more like a fool than ever. "She didn't have stars in her eyes because I didn't sleep with her. We aren't married. We won't ever be married."

"You told her that, right?"

"Yes."

"And she still agreed to help?"

"She agreed to help regardless." Lillian had simply looked

at him with her heart in her eyes, confused, hurt, and so beautiful he'd wanted to take her in his arms and kiss it all away. But he couldn't. It wasn't right. She deserved better.

"No!"

"What?"

"Tell me you did not sneak out before she woke up."

Donovan felt the heat of embarrassment run up the back of his neck. He hunched his shoulders and trained his eye on the horizon.

"You did," McCormick said, amazement in his tone. "You snuck out like a thief in the night."

The sound of their horses' hooves hitting dirt filled Donovan's ears. A hawk shrieked overhead. Heat from the sun hit his back, baking him.

"No, I spoke to her before I left this morning," Donovan said. It would have been easier to slip away, but he'd done what he thought was the right thing. He'd hurt her outright and told her why.

"What'd you tell her?"

"That I don't intend to sleep with her. That sex is a stupid thing to do."

"I'd have never believed it," Mac went on. "The great Donovan loving a woman and then leaving her cold."

"She's smart," Donovan grumbled. "She'll figure out it was for the best."

"Yeah, whose best? Yours or hers?"

"Hers." He shot his friend a heavy look. "The last thing she needs is to get pregnant."

"You mean the last thing you need." McCormick whistled low. "What did you tell her?"

"I told her about Susan," Donovan said. "I laid it all out."

"And?"

"And she said I wasn't responsible for her. That she made her own decisions."

"And?"

"She said she didn't get along well with others so it was all right that I wasn't going to stick around."

"Shoot, it was not all right." Mac shook his head and spit. "You don't use a woman like Lillian and then tell her you didn't mean it." He paused and eyed Donovan. "Did you at least tell her thank you?"

Silence wafted around them. Donovan felt more like a heel than ever.

"You didn't, did you? Christ, Donovan, you should turn around right now and go back and talk to her."

"It's too late," Donovan muttered. He hated how Mac's words grated raw against his conscience. "It will be dark by the time I get back to town. She'll have locked up again. If I crawl in her window now, she really will shoot me."

Lillian was too busy to dwell on much of what had happened. She had just enough time to hang the bedding out to dry before another customer came in wanting to order something for their Founders Day celebration. Then she had to deal with her supplier, who demanded to see Donovan.

It took Mr. Huckabee explaining that Donovan had told him he was looking at a couple of investments and wouldn't be back until Saturday before the supplier agreed that Lillian could sign the order.

What a mess. Before Donovan had showed up no one questioned her actions. Now all they did was ask about him. What was it he wanted? When would he be back? Was she sure she wanted to keep working now that Donovan had come home?

Lillian closed the shop promptly at eight and went out back to haul her bedding in off the line.

"Yoo-hoo." The trill sound of Mrs. Huckabee's voice had Lillian grinding her back teeth. She plastered a smile on her face.

"Hello, Mrs. Huckabee. How are you?"

"Fine, fine." She stopped short to watch Lillian take her laundry down. "Bedding, I see." Lillian hated the sly smile that crossed the older woman's face. "Nothing like having your man around, is there, dear? Especially a man as virile as yours." She sighed.

Lillian searched for something to talk about besides the fact that she had washed sheets. "Are you ready for the Founders Day celebration?"

"Oh, yes, I've been ready for a month." Mrs. Huckabee's keen gaze never left Lillian's sheets.

Nosy so-and-so, Lillian thought.

"How about you?"

"All ready," Lillian said. "I finished my dress this afternoon."

"Has it been slow at the store? I mean, we saw your man riding off again this morning."

"He's looking at possible mining sites." Lillian folded the sheets. "The store is doing well, but Donovan likes to keep an eye out for new investments."

"He'll be busy once you start having children and can no longer run the store," Mrs. Huckabee predicted. "What is he thinking, getting into mining?"

"He's thinking about the future." Lillian put the folded sheets into her basket. "A mine would give us the revenue to expand the store. Wouldn't it be nice to have a department store in Silverton?"

"My, do you think the town could support one?" The older woman tilted her head thoughtfully.

"Donovan could make anything work." Lillian lifted the full basket onto her hip. What she really meant was that she could make it work. Lillian had been thinking about expanding for some time. She had the cash saved up. It was simply a matter of demographics. She wanted to make sure Silverton wouldn't disappear once the silver mines emptied.

"Oh, do keep an eye on your money, dear." Mrs. Huckabee stepped closer and leaned in as if to spread a secret. "I hear that someone may be passing counterfeit bills around town."

"Really?" Lillian lifted an eyebrow. "How?"

"Art Miller over at the feed store passed the word that he'd seen a phony bill. We're trying to keep it between the townsfolk. Surely some stranger is attempting to stick us with false money."

"What did Mr. Sandler at the bank have to say about that?"

"He said he'd be sure and have enough reserve, should we insist on cashing in all the paper money."

"For what? Gold? Don't you think it would be awkward to carry around all that heavy coinage?"

"Mr. Huckabee said he'd settle for silver, being as the price is good right now. I heard that Mr. Miller is putting up a notice that he is accepting only gold and silver now. That will show anyone who thinks they can fool us."

"What about the ranchers?" Lillian asked. "Most of them carry paper bills."

"Well, they'll have to trade them in at the bank, now won't they?"

Lillian worried her bottom lip. "Won't that cause a run on the bank?"

The older woman leaned in close, her gray curls bobbing. "I heard tell that there is a shipment coming in from back East on Saturday. If I were you, I would turn in any paper bills you have for silver only." She patted Lillian's arm. "Can't say I didn't give you fair warning." She winked. "Enjoy your clean sheets." Then she waved and walked off.

Lillian figured the whole town would know she had washed her sheets before the sun set.

She walked into the back room, put the basket down on the table, and turned to lock the door. It pushed open before she could close it.

"Hey, Red." Bart Johnson stuck his foot between the door and the jamb so that she couldn't slam it in his face. "Where's your man?" He pushed his way into the room.

"What do you want?" Lillian's heart rate sped up. Bart Johnson was a dangerous man, and this was the first time he'd gone so far as to trespass on her property.

"There's a lot of things I want, Red." Bart moved restlessly around the room. His hands rested on his hips, close to the gun in his holster. "Where's your husband?"

Lillian had her shotgun under the desk, but Bart was between her and the desk. The curtain was behind her. She could bolt to the front but she figured it wouldn't do much good. She had already closed up, locking the doors and closing the shutters.

"Funny how he's always leaving you."

Lillian stood her ground as he touched a lock of her hair that had slid from its bounds and ran it through his fingers.

"He's due in for dinner." Lillian turned with Bart. She'd learned long ago it was never good to have your back to a wild animal. Besides, now she had her back to the desk.

"Yeah, good." Bart grabbed a chair by the potbelly stove in the center of the room and sat down. His beady eyes looked at her in a way that made her skin crawl. "Him and me are going to have some words."

"Donovan is a busy man. I'm sure whatever you have to say can wait until morning."

"Nope." Bart spit. She frowned. Now she was going to have to mop the floor. "I'm talking to him tonight." Bart took his pistol out of the holster and ran his hand along the barrel. "Like I said . . . him and me, we're going to have words."

Lillian's mind raced. It was like facing a rattling snake. She would have to move slow and careful and above all be smarter than Bart. She took a couple of steps back. Let him think she was afraid of his gun. "Put that thing away," she said. "There's no need for firearms in my home."

"What'cha gonna do about it?" Bart asked with a gleam in his eye. "Call the sheriff? 'Cause he's out with the mayor looking over the Founders Day decorations in the town square. Seems to me, the town square is far enough away, they won't hear you scream."

Cold sweat trickled down Lillian's back. She pretended to stumble back against the desk. "Why would I need to scream?"

Bart stood up so fast he knocked the chair over. "Because I'm going to have some fun tonight."

"I told you, Donovan will be here any moment." Her hands groped for the gun behind her.

Bart grinned. "Won't he be surprised to find you cuckolded him. Might even make him downright furious." He took a step toward her.

She wrapped her hands around the shotgun and drew it out in front of her. Her fingers clicked the trigger. "Don't come a step closer."

"Or what?" Bart asked. "You going to shoot me? I don't think so. A little thing like you might catch a man off guard with her umbrella, but this time I'm prepared. He pointed his gun at her. I'm bettin' you won't shoot. If you do shoot, I'm bettin' I've got better aim. So, who do you think has better aim, darling? You or me?"

"Me." Lillian lifted the rifle to her shoulder. "Now get out before I shoot you."

He laughed and took a step closer. "You ain't got nothing but buckshot in that thing. Buckshot ain't gonna stop a man."

"Well, now, let's find out." Lillian squeezed the trigger. The vibration rattled through her shoulder and into her back teeth. The scent of sulfur filled the air, followed by Bart Johnson's scream. His gun rattled to the floor as he clutched his bloody arm against his chest.

"You shot me," he said, pain and anger in his eyes.

"I didn't kill you." She adjusted the bolt to drop the cartridge and bring in a new one.

"You should have!" He lunged toward her. She pulled the trigger a second time. This time, she didn't wait. She moved to the back door. Her ears rang. Her nostrils filled with acrid smoke. Bart was on his knees holding his shoulder. Pain and hate was in his eyes.

He swore and tried to get up. Lillian opened the back door and ran into something very hard. She looked up into the face of a very dirty, very ugly man and, for the first time in her life, Lillian knew terror.

Chapter Fourteen

His bedroll was hard and rocky under the cold sky. The sound of a small fire crackled near his feet. It didn't give off heat, just a little light and enough scent to keep the bears away. Donovan put his hands under his head and stared up at the star-studded darkness.

The day had been another total loss. The lack of progress on the case frustrated him to no end. The only clue they had was the bill he'd found after the weekend's wild rush of miners.

Mac poked the fire, stirring the ashes. "We could spend another two weeks out here and find nothing," he said. "There's too much territory to cover."

"What about the silver changers? Did you ever get anything there?"

"I couldn't get anyone to let me in on it. Seems they are selective. Smart actually. They only silver change a handful of miners per town. That way no one gets suspicious."

Smart and careful didn't usually go hand in hand with criminal intent. "Yes, but how much money can you make that way?"

"More than you think, if they're centrally located." Mac picked up a stick and drew on the ground. "Say there are a thousand miners in a four-county area. Now, you money change a hundred. They think they're getting a deal because you're paying three times the going rate."

"When in fact you're getting silver for the price of paper," Donovan concluded.

"If anyone finds out the bills aren't real, they can't come back and get you because it was all done under the table."

"Smart."

"Smarter still if you were working with a banker," Mac pointed out.

A banker who was back in town. A town where Donovan had sown the seeds of doubt. A feeling of dread snaked down his spine. "Do you think Fred Sandler is in on it?"

"Could be," Mac said and settled into his bedroll. "You did say he was the major money changer for the town."

"Darn it." Donovan sat up.

"What?" Mac eyed him from under his hat.

"I gave one of the locals a heads-up on the counterfeit cash."

"Right, and all the businessmen will know what to look for." Mac's eyes sparkled in the faint firelight.

"If Sandler is in on it . . ."

"Then he'll know you're on to him."

"And Lillian isn't safe." Donovan rolled up his bedding. "I'm going back."

Mac put his arm on Donovan's shoulder. "It's late, and it's dark."

"She could be in trouble." Panic was a feeling Donovan would never forget. One he'd hoped to never feel again after Susan died.

"You said yourself she'd shoot you if you came in after dark. I'm sure she can handle herself alone for one night."

Donovan couldn't shake the overwhelming urge to rush to Lillian's side. "I'd rather not take the chance."

"Then I'm not letting you go back alone." Mac got up and tightened his gunbelt, adjusted his hat.

"It'll make for a heck of a long night," Donovan pointed out, feeling stupid for panicking and causing his partner to lose a good night's sleep.

"Shoot, somebody's got to watch your back." Mac's white teeth shone in the dark. "Otherwise who's going to write the report for headquarters?"

"You're writing it." Donovan picked up his saddle. "You know I hate paperwork."

"Good thing I can write." Mac poured water over the small

blaze. The sound of fire hissing as it died and then the scent of water on ashes filled the air.

Donovan realized that he actually felt better. Leaving Lillian had bothered him more than he realized. It was probably stupid to ride through the night, but at least this way he'd know for sure she was all right.

"The bitch shot me," Bart whined. "Twice."

"Let me go!" Lillian demanded as the big ugly man held her tight. His meaty hand wrapped around her forearm like a vise. Two other men were with him. One smaller and balding, the other Lillian could barely see, but something about him was familiar.

"You realize half the town is headed this way." Lillian recognized Fred Sandler's voice. "Get her out of here and fast."

"No!" For the first time in her life, Lillian regretted being so small. No matter how hard she kicked and hit, the big guy didn't let go. In fact, he picked her up as if she were a small animal and tucked her up over his shoulders, carrying her like a lamb.

Lillian bucked and squirmed but could not dislodge herself as he strode quickly through the yard and behind the outhouse. Screaming her head off in hopes that someone would hear, Lillian suddenly saw stars. The pain was unexpected and took her breath away.

"Stay quiet," the big man growled. He ducked inside the small stable. It was dark and warm. Lillian's stomach lurched at the pain along her cheek.

He covered her mouth with his hand. She tried to bite him when he hit her again and stuffed a dirty handkerchief in her mouth. The scent of horses and straw combined with the strong sweat of the man who held her like a small animal.

The cloth in her mouth tasted like coal dust and sweat. She squirmed to remove it, but he held her hands in one giant paw so tight she could not move. She could hear the man's breath coming in and out and the odd sound of horses moving nearby. He moved near the wall, and she could see through the cracks in the planking.

A crowd arrived. The banker came around the corner as if he too had just come from home. Some of the men had guns. One or two had bats. The crowd funneled into the light that came from her opened back door. She could hear the murmurs of the crowd as they worked to determine what had happened.

"What is it, Henry?" Mrs. Huckabee said, so close that Lillian knew she stood beside the stables. "Is Lillian all right? Who was shooting?"

"The back door was open, but no one is home," the barber said. "I was one of the first inside. Looks as if she brought the laundry inside and went to close the door. Someone must have forced their way in."

"Oh, no." Mrs. Huckabee gasped. "What about the gun-shots?"

"Someone was hit, that's for sure. There was blood and what looked like a struggle."

"Do you think someone shot Mr. West?"

"There's no sign of a body or anyone hurt, so the sheriff thinks it might be the Wests got a shot or two off before they were taken."

"Taken? As in kidnapped?"

"Yep, kidnapped all right." Mr. Huckabee's voice boomed in her ears.

Lillian's brain shouted that she was right here, right behind them. She kicked and bucked, hoping that maybe she could get the big guy to bump into the wall. That someone would come to see what the noise was. But the big man shook her until her teeth rattled. He grabbed a rope off his belt and hog-tied her. His hands gripped her so tight she could not feel her hands or feet.

"What was that?" Lillian struggled harder.

"What, dear?"

"I thought I heard something. Do you think the kidnappers are still around?"

Lillian went wild. She pounded her head against his shoulder. Used her elbows to jab him in the side. She had to make a noise. The big man grabbed her by the throat and squeezed so hard Lillian's world darkened. She went limp. He let go, and she was able to take a painful breath.

"The men are searching the premises now," Mr. Huckabee said outside the stable. "But I want you to go inside and keep the door locked, do you hear me?"

"I most certainly will," Mrs. Huckabee agreed. Their voices grew farther away, and Lillian's energy drained. Her only hope was that someone would search the stables.

The hope didn't last long, as the big guy made his way out the back side with Lillian thrown over his shoulder like a sack of feed. He looked both ways and then cut across the empty space to another building. Weaving his way through the shadowed backyards to the edge of town, he stopped next to a dilapidated wagon.

Bart Johnson waited there with a large burlap bag in his hands. Lillian fought tooth and nail, but the men merely grimaced and stuffed her into the bag, tying the end around her feet. She was tossed unceremoniously into the back of the wagon. The fall took her breath away, jarring her already sore body.

The wagon lifted and rocked. The only sound was the horse's hooves as they hit dirt and drove off.

Donovan and McCormick arrived in town as the sun shot pale pink light over the tops of the mountains. A crowd buzzed around the general store, and his stomach twisted with fear. Was he too late?

"Thank God, Mr. West!" Pete ran up beside the horses. "We thought maybe you were the one who was shot."

Fear, slick and black, slid through his veins. "Whoa, slow down, what are you talking about?" Donovan jumped off his horse and led him through the crowd.

"The whole town heard gunshots last night coming from the general store. When we got there the back door was wide open, and the lamplight showed blood in the back room."

"Blood? What about Lillian?" Donovan's heartbeat sped up. Panic rose in his throat. He started to run toward the store.

"We don't know!" The kid ran with him. "There wasn't a

single soul found. Just the blood. We thought maybe someone had done you in."

Someone had Lillian. Donovan tossed the reins toward the kid and hurried up the front porch.

"What happened?" Donovan demanded of the grave-faced townsmen gathered. "Where's Lillian?" He pushed through the crowd.

"Slow down there, son." Sherriff Mann put his hand on Donovan's shoulder. Donovan shook it off.

"What's going on?" Mac asked. Donovan realized for the first time that his partner had been beside him the whole way.

"We're not sure," the sheriff said. "We were in the town square last night when we heard what sounded like a shotgun go off. The back door was open, and it looks like she put up a mighty struggle."

"Lillian!" Donovan could no longer contain the emotions inside him. He raced to the back room. The place was a mess. Blood pooled on the floor. The desk where she kept her loaded shotgun had its door hanging open.

"Best we can figure, someone burst in on her." The sheriff nodded toward the basket full of folded bedding. "She must have been bringing laundry in off the line."

"Who?" The word came out in a croak. Donovan had his suspicions and needed to know what the sherriff knew.

"We're not sure. Last person we know saw her is Mrs. Huckabee. She was here chatting with Lillian after eight," the sheriff said. "But she left her when your missus went inside. Best we can tell, he was either lying in wait or pushed his way through. The door's got a splinter." The lawman nodded toward the door.

Mac walked over and checked it out. "Looks pushed in."

Donovan sent Mac a look. It had to have been the counterfeit ring. He'd bet his best pocket watch Bart Johnson was involved.

"There was no mob," the sheriff said.

"Sheriff thought maybe someone came after you an' got Lillian instead," Mr. Huckabee piped up.

Donovan realized just exactly how stupid he'd been. "Someone wanted me and got Lillian instead." Johnson had already had his suspicions. It wouldn't be hard to guess it was Donovan who'd spread the word about the counterfeit bill to the other business owners. He should have never left her alone.

"She can take care of herself," Mac said pointedly.

Donovan shot his friend a heavy look. "Lillian kept a loaded shotgun in the desk drawer. The one hanging off its hinge. This chair is also out of place." He walked over to the desk. "I think she got the gun and pointed it at whoever was in the chair." He stood in front of the desk and held a pretend gun to his shoulder, eyeing the chair. "It would explain the blood."

"Keep in mind how small she is." Mac lowered Donovan's arms. "She would be shooting from here."

Whoever it was must have stepped forward. Pacing off the distance to the chair and then the area of blood spill, he looked at Donovan. "She knew him."

"How do you figure?" Donovan asked, narrowing his eyes.

"She didn't shoot to kill." Mac held out his hand. "I bet she shot his hand." He drew out his gun and pointed it at Donovan. Then he nodded. "She shot him in the hand."

"So someone had a gun to her?" The sheriff chewed a toothpick and eyed the scenario. "If she knew him, he wasn't friendly."

"So, what, he was stealing something?" Mr. Huckabee asked. "'Cause if there's a robber around, our womenfolk need to know."

"No, like I said, nothing's missing," the sheriff said.

"Nothing but Lillian," Donovan growled.

"Nothing but your lovely wife," the sheriff agreed. "Now, why don't you tell me just who would want to take your wife?"

"Someone looking to get back at me," Donovan said. He eyed the crowd. "Whoever she shot would not be able to carry her off with his arm mangled."

"Unless he had help," Mac said.

"He had to have help. It couldn't have been more than two

minutes from the time we heard the second blast to the time we swarmed the shop."

"And you saw no one." Donovan ground his back teeth.

"Well, we saw half the town come running," the sheriff said. "Pretty much every man in town responded."

"None of them were shot," the barber pointed out. "So it had to be someone we don't know so well."

"What about Doc?" Mac asked. "Anyone report getting shot?"

"No injuries came in to see me." Doc leaned against the door. "Not even that little lady of yours."

"You think Lillian might have shot herself?" Donovan scowled at the absurdity of that.

"Was she a good shot?" Doc asked.

"She is a good shot," Donovan said. "Besides, if she shot herself, where the heck is she?" He eyed the steps. He frowned and pushed passed the men, went upstairs, and opened the apartment door. It was quiet as a tomb. The windows were closed and locked. He went into the bedroom. The bed had been stripped. Everything was neat and tidy. There was no sign of Lillian.

It was a good bet the counterfeiters had her and planned to use her to get to him. Well, they would get him all right, and then they would rue the day they had messed with him and his.

"We'll find her."

Donovan glanced over his shoulder at Mac standing in the doorway between the bedroom and the parlor. "I should have stayed here with her."

"Let's not dwell on 'shoulds' right now," Mac said. "Come on, let's go out back and look around. There has to be some sign of struggle. Knowing your Lillian, more than one of these pieces of dung is hurt." He slapped Donovan on the shoulder and pushed him to the door. "I hope she makes them all real sorry they ever ran into her."

Lillian never hurt so bad in her life. Her body felt as if she had been run over by a stagecoach. She opened her eyes to the dim light filtering through burlap. The scent of raw burlap and feed filled her nostrils. When she sneezed, her head felt as if it exploded.

For the life of her, she couldn't figure out where she was or why she hurt so badly.

The rolling and tossing stopped suddenly. Lillian's fuzzy brain cleared. She remember exactly what happened and could not believe that she had passed out somewhere in the darkness.

"What are we going to do with her?" she heard Bart Johnson say. His voice came from her left.

"We can use her to lure West to us." Fred Sandler's voice came from a distance above Bart's, leading Lillian to believe that he was on horseback.

"How will he know we have her?"

"I left him a few clues. He'll figure it out. Now, get her out of the wagon and lock her in the cellar. I've got to get back to town and keep an eye on things there."

"What about me?" Bart whined. "I'm full of buckshot. Can you send Doc up to pull it out?"

"You'll have to do it yourself. You left too much blood in the back room. Now everyone knows whoever did this was shot. They're expecting someone to see the doc. That someone can't be you."

"But I'm hurting. I could die."

"There's whiskey aplenty in the cabin. You'll figure it out. If not, well, then you'll die." She heard the jangle of a horse tossing its head. "I'll be back. We'll work out what we're going to do then."

She heard the horse gallop off. Someone grabbed her feet and dragged her to the edge of the wagon. Splinters stuck her through the burlap. She bit her lip so as not to groan. The last thing she wanted was for them to know she was awake. Maybe if she were quiet enough they would think she was dead and leave her unguarded.

Big hands took ahold of her ankles and flung her up and over a broad shoulder like a bag of feed. She couldn't help the sound that escaped her when her middle hit broad muscle.

A big hand patted her backside, and she wanted to bite him. Instead, she counted his steps and paid attention to the light and shadows that made it through the burlap. He took thirty steps, climbing. The shadows deepened. She must be in the pines. A door creaked open, and he moved down into cool blackness. It smelled like dirt and churned-up must.

"I say we leave her in the bag," Bart sniveled. "The bitch darn near killed me."

"No skin off my nose," came the deep reply. She felt as if she were flying through the air, and then she hit the ground hard. It knocked the wind out of her, and she worked not to panic. She heard them climb up eight, maybe nine, stairs. Then there was the bang of a wooden door and the darkness was complete.

Chapter Fifteen

Mccormick was the best tracker Donovan had ever known, and he'd known his fair share. He swallowed the pounding feelings of regret and anger and followed his friend's lead.

"Any trail they might have left near the back door was erased by the sheer number of men milling about," Mac said from his squatted position. "Best I can tell, people have been coming and going from this doorway for hours." He eyed the yard. "Let's say you knew you had only a few seconds to snatch the girl and get away."

"She had to be unconscious," Donovan said. "She's too much of a fighter to be pulled along."

"Okay, so you knock her unconscious. That takes a few seconds, cuts into your time, but then you throw her over your shoulder and go."

"Right."

"If it were me, I'd head diagonal, toward the stables." Mac stood, pointed, and eyed the length of his arm. "If you go straight back to the outhouse, you risk being too obvious."

"The fence on the right prevents you from going that way quickly," Donovan chimed in.

He walked toward the stables, watching the ground carefully. Once they moved three yards from the back door, the number of footprints in the dry dirt lessoned, finally showing four. Two made a straight line toward the stables. Two others seemed to simply wander over that way.

"Who owns the stable?" Mac asked.

"The Huckabees."

"So, these two sets of prints could belong to the barber and his wife. See how this one has swirls around it? Probably her skirts. Plus the shoe size is smaller."

"These prints are bigger." Donovan squatted down. "One side here is deeper than the other." He looked up at Mac. "Probably the guy carrying Lillian."

The two made their way to the stables and cautiously drew their guns. "I doubt he's still in there," Mac said.

"Doesn't hurt to be prepared." The two nodded and slowly entered the stables. It was a small two-stall building, mostly lean-to in appearance. The roof was solidly stitched, but the building sides were unchinked. The floor was covered in straw.

The two men carefully checked the entire space. All they found were a couple of barn cats and a horse in each stall.

"Looks like he slid right inside." Mac got down on one knee and looked at the ground close to the wall. "There were two of them, standing right here." He stood up. "They could see everything that was happening at the back of the store."

"Lillian had to be unconscious, or she would have screamed her head off," Donovan concluded. Anger rose inside him in waves. Where was she? Was she all right? He swore he'd kill them if they harmed her in any way.

"They probably waited until most of the attention was on the inside of the store." Mac walked to the back of the stables. "They went out this way."

Donovan put his gun in his holster and followed his friend. Behind the stables was a thin alley that ran the length of the entire town. "It wouldn't be hard to stay in the shadows here and out of sight."

"Probably strolled out right under the noses of the entire town."

"It was dark and the back buildings provided good cover." The two men followed the alley to its end at the edge of the small town. There they found wagon tracks.

"They took off from here."

"I'm going back to get my horse," Donovan said grimly.

"Bring mine. I'll walk down the road a bit and see if I can tell what direction they were going."

Donovan nodded and headed out to the main street down the middle to the feed store where Pete held their horses.

"Hey, West," Fred Sandler called out. Donovan looked over his shoulder and spied the banker coming out of the bank. "Sorry to hear about your wife," he said. "I hope she's okay. Any idea who could have done such a dastardly thing?"

"None," Donovan said. "I've got to go."

"Sure, sure," Sandler said. "Listen, you need anything, anything at all, you let me know."

"Thanks." Donovan ignored the concern in the man's eyes and took off toward the feed store. If the banker was behind this, he was audacious enough to come out looking concerned. That meant he felt secure. Donovan hoped to keep it that way, at least for the time being.

"Pete's bringing your horses out," Art said, when Donovan stepped up on the walk outside the feed store. "We saw you coming. Figured you might have tracked the buggers."

"We did, thanks," Donovan said.

"Need a posse to go with you?" Art asked. "I can have at least five men saddled in less than five minutes."

"McCormick and I can handle it." Donovan took his reins and stepped up into his saddle. His body ached from the long ride through the night, but he ignored it. Finding Lillian was his only goal right now, and he'd do whatever it took to get the job done.

"You think this might have something to do with that bill you showed me?" Art asked.

Donovan studied the old man. His pale blue eyes were as sharp as daggers. "Yeah, but don't let that get around."

Art nodded. "We'll keep an extra eye out then. Sandler told me there was a shipment of gold coming in Saturday. I'll talk to the sheriff about having an extra guard put out."

"Not a bad idea," Donovan said.

Pete came around the side of the building with a concerned look on his face.

"What is it?" Art asked his son.

"I found this." Pete handed Donovan a folded sheet of paper. He looked at Donovan with concern. "It was in the stall where I stabled your horse. Is that some sort of ransom?"

Donovan opened the paper. Inside was a thickly scrawled note telling him he was to go up to the old Foster mine alone if he ever wanted to see Lillian alive again.

"West?" Art asked with concern.

Donovan carefully closed the note and put it in his shirt pocket. "Whoever has Lillian wants me up at the Foster mine." He leaned down so that the conversation didn't carry. "Where the heck is that?"

"About five miles straight up that west mountain," Art said. "I'll tell the sheriff to send a posse."

"Give me until tomorrow morning," Donovan said. "If I'm not back down by then, send your posse. In the meantime, try to keep the ladies calm."

"Will do," Art said.

Donovan ground his back teeth tight and galloped toward the end of town where he'd pick up Mac. His insides had gone stone cold at the sight of the note. He was responsible for Lillian's welfare. Whoever was behind this knew he was in town. Knew he was looking at the counterfeit ring. That meant they were part of the town's inner circle. Art would figure that out and keep a close watch. But it was Donovan who'd be sure whoever did this knew he was the one who was going to kill them.

Getting the binding off her ankles took the longest. By now the knots were tied impossibly deep. Her fingers and toes were numb from the cold and it was frustratingly dark. Too dark to do anything but try to feel her way out of her binding.

She wore the burlap sack as a shawl. It hadn't taken but a couple of pulls to separate the bag from the tie. If only she had a knife or a pair of scissors. She'd cut the sucker off her ankles.

Cold, tired, and beyond thirsty, Lillian stopped and listened for any sound of another human. She heard rustling in another corner and shook her head. It was probably a rodent. She hated rodents, but as long as it left her alone, she'd leave it alone.

When you grew up in an orphanage, you learned early on not to be squeamish.

Why had she not thought to carry a knife with her? Before Donovan, she'd kept one in her apron pocket, if for no other reason than to cut strings when she packaged up goods people bought. When she hurt her ankle, Donovan had taken that job from her, and he kept the knife under the counter—where it was at this very moment.

It didn't do to waste time cursing the darkness. She had recognized the banker's voice, which meant they weren't planning on letting her go. According to Bart, it was Donovan they wanted. She was merely a means to an end.

If they hoped she was bait enough to bring Donovan running, they would soon find out how wrong they were. She wasn't about to wait around for that moment. If she had to guess, she'd figure they wanted Donovan because he had warned the town about the counterfeit money. That meant that the banker and Bart Johnson were somehow mixed up with the men who were making the counterfeit money. The very men Donovan and Kane had come to Silverton to investigate. A lot of things were at stake here. Her life was the least of it.

Lillian worked her ankles raw, trying to stretch the binding so that she could slip one foot out. If it weren't for the leather on her shoe tops, she'd probably be bleeding.

There was only one thing left to do. She bent down and chewed on the rope that bound her ankles. The hemp was rough and lashed at her lips and gums, but it was chew or give up, and Lillian had never been the type to give up.

"The Foster mine was the first big silver strike in the area," Mac said as they rode their horses straight up the mountain. "It was also the first to peter out."

"So it's abandoned."

"Supposed to be. From what I heard, it's now a big cavern.

Some of the miners take refuge in it when there is an early snowstorm."

"Perfect place for a printing press. The earth would dampen the sound."

"And they are close enough to several mining towns that they could easily trade cash for silver, and then silver for real cash in another town."

"Even better if they are working for a bank." Donovan narrowed his eyes and scowled. "Sandler was right there asking if we had any idea who might have done this to Lillian."

"You think he knows who we are?"

"No. What he does know is that I got the town looking for counterfeit cash." Donovan shook his head. "He even thanked me for alerting everyone. Keeps him solid, he said."

"So he knows it's you."

"Yeah, and he was one of the first men on scene when Lillian went missing."

"Convenient."

"I thought so."

"Maybe it's more than a little counterfeit money," Mac mused.

"What do you mean?"

"Well, the counterfeit stuff had made them some money, but not a whole lot."

"It's too easy to be caught if you stay in one place and spread it around," Donovan agreed.

"And these crooks aren't moving."

"So there's a bigger plot?" In his experience, there was always more to it.

"Think about it," Mac said. "You let the townspeople know what to look for. What was the banker's reaction?"

"He swore that he could cover, in gold, any rush on the bank."

"And how is he doing that?"

"Having a shipment brought in Saturday."

"A shipment of gold, enough to cover the accounts for the county." Mac spit to the side of the road.

"That's a heck of a lot of gold," Donovan agreed.

"Even with four men guarding it."

"So, it's not about the money at all." Donovan sucked on his teeth. "It's about the gold."

"And this thing with Lillian is a diversion," Mac said. "Hate to call it that, but it does take everyone's mind off the fact that there is a—"

"Great deal of gold on its way to be stolen."

They stopped their horses. Donovan eyed his friend. "I can deal with this from here. Why don't you head over to Leadville and telegraph the Denver office. Give them a heads-up and see what they want us to do."

"What about Lillian?"

"I got her into this mess, and I'll get her out if it's the last thing I do."

Mac spit again and narrowed his eyes. "After I contact the Denver office, I'll send a posse up to the Foster mine. My guess is they'll find the printing press sans plates and enough counterfeit cash to make them feel like heroes. This was a setup, Donovan."

"Yeah. So where is Lillian then?"

"Somewhere close by." Mac scanned the horizon. "The banker got back too quick to have taken her far."

"I'll start from the mine. Might be a clue there to lead me in the right direction."

"I can stay and help you track," Mac offered.

"Our job is saving that gold," Donovan said with fierce determination. "Do the job."

"And if you get hurt chasing Lillian?"

"It's the least I deserve."

Mac reached over and patted him on the back. "I fully expect you back in Silverton for the dance on Saturday."

Donovan nodded grimly. "I fully intend on being there."

Lillian nearly cried with relief when she felt the binding give. Her mouth tasted of blood and raw hemp. She stood up and stamped her feet. The numbness in her toes gave way to sharp needle tingles. Her head hurt at the new elevation, but she was free. Standing was even more odd than sitting, as it was so dark she had no idea where the ceiling was. She reached up and her fingertips brushed dirt. So the big man must have had to duck to get her down here. Maybe he simply threw her down. It certainly felt like he'd thrown her down.

She moved in the dark with her hands out in front of her, hoping to find the stairs.

Within four strides her hands hit a dirt wall. She blew out a breath. Her nostrils filled with the musty scent of dirt and roots. She eased her way along the edge of the wall. Sooner or later she was bound to run into the stairs.

Chapter Sixteen

Lillian had not been so cold since she was a small child found wandering in the streets. She dreamed of her little tin bathtub and warm water scented by a sliver of violet essence soap.

She had to be covered with dirt and grime. Not that it mattered, since she was still in total darkness. All sense of time was gone. Her luck was running badly. Seems she had followed the wall in the wrong direction. It took her what felt like countless hours of easing around unidentifiable boxes, old burlap sacks, and things hanging.

Countless spiderwebs brushed across her face. She sneezed and wished for a cold drink of fresh well water.

No one came to check on her. No one opened the door. When she hit her third wall with no stairs, she sat down on the ground and cried.

It didn't matter. No one saw her. She was hungry, thirsty, tired, and hurting in places she didn't want to think about. She placed the burlap on her shoulders and placed her hands on the wall. She had made an arrow in the dirt before she stopped so she wouldn't spend more hours going the wrong way. "Just one more wall and then we have to reach stairs."

She didn't go but a couple of feet before her shins bumped something hard. Tears welled at the pain, but she recovered soon enough when her hands hit a railing.

Stairs. She had found the stairs.

Elation and a renewed sense of purpose filled her as she climbed with one hand on the rail and the other out in front of her searching for the door.

She found it at the top of the tenth stair. The door sloped at a steep angle above her. She found the edge and ran her fingers along it, looking for a hinge or handle. The handle was just an inch or so above her head. She grabbed it and pushed up, but the door didn't budge.

Cellars were built into the sides of the mountains. Doors generally were steeply hung and heavy, to keep marauding bears and other creatures out.

"Well, at least the bears and cougars won't eat me." She sighed long and hard. Either it was nighttime outside or the door was so well built it didn't have a crack in the chinking.

She sat down to think. It was then that she heard it. Someone was near the door. Lillian stood up and hurried down the stairs. Foolish, she thought. She should have armed herself earlier with one of those metal things hanging from the ceiling. But all she had thought about was getting out of the dark.

Now she scurried back into the blackness and managed to get under the steps when the sound of chain rattled over the wood. The door had been chained. Even if she could have raised it up, she could not have been able to keep it open high enough to crawl out.

She searched around for something, anything to use to protect herself. Her hands landed on a large rock. She wrapped her hand around the smooth surface until two-thirds of the rock stuck out. It would do as a makeshift hammer. She stuffed her arm behind her back as the door *woof*ed and creaked and groaned open.

Surprisingly, the darkness didn't get any better with the opening of the door. Which meant it must be nighttime. But what night? Had she been down here only a few hours or had it been longer?

"Lillian? Lillian, are you down there?" It sounded like Donovan whispering. She held her ground in case it was a trick.

She heard boots hit the stairs and come halfway down. "Shoot, it's darker than an unlit mine down here," he muttered. "Lillian! Honey, it's me, Donovan. Please come to my voice if you can hear me."

Her heart sped up. Donovan? Was he alone?

"Dadgummit," Donovan muttered under his breath. "I hate dark mines. Listen, it's not safe enough to light a lamp." He took two more stairs.

Lillian raised her rock.

"Honey, I swear it's me and I'm alone. Come out."

"If it's you, really you," she whispered, "how did you get here without anyone noticing?"

She heard his boots turn. So he knew her general location. His voice came from right in front of her, causing her heart to leap. "Honey, I'm smarter than these idiots." He paused. "Look, I figure you're cold, thirsty, and probably armed with something. Please don't hurt me."

She giggled at the raw truth in his tone. It was her Donovan. Relief had her rushing out from under the stairs and smack into his arms.

"Aw, darlin'." He gathered her close. He smelled good. Warm and safe and like her man. She clung to him. The emotional relief had hot, wet tears running down her checks. He held her to him like a precious object. Her face was held tight against his chest. She felt the leather of his jacket and the soft flannel of the shirt underneath.

"What took you so long?" she asked, tipping her head up for his kiss. The kiss was strong and sweet. But far too short.

"Let's get out of here." He bent down and picked her up, carrying her up the stairs and out into the cold night air. The sky was black and crystal clear. Thousands of stars filled the sky. Tree branches rustled as he carried her carefully away from the mouth of the cellar. He put her down yards away and held his finger to his lips. Lillian nodded. She didn't need to be told to be quiet. She was pretty certain no one suspected that she was escaping.

Donovan grabbed her hand and pulled her through the trees in a dizzying zigzag pattern. Her lungs burned and her heart raced. She picked up her skirts with her free hand to keep them from catching on the undergrowth.

After what seemed forever, they came upon Donovan's horse wandering free, eating what tidbits it could find under the trees.

Without a word, Donovan picked her up and chucked her in front of the saddle. The big horse moved restlessly under her. She grabbed its mane to hang on and then leaned over the fine neck, patting it and whispering how lovely a horse he was.

The saddle rocked as Donovan climbed up behind her and swung his leg over. He grabbed the reins on either side of her and turned the horse's head in a direction away from the cabin.

The horse picked up their sense of urgency and strained to hurry. Donovan kept a tight rein. Lillian knew it was too dark to be running away willy-nilly, even though that's what her instincts told her to do.

They rode careful but steady for a long time before Donovan eased up on the reins and nudged her with a canteen. "Here, drink this before you pass out."

Lillian didn't give a fig about manners. She grabbed the canteen and greedily chugged what she could of the contents.

"Hold up there, love. Too much will make you sick and we don't have time for that." He dragged the canteen away from her. He capped it and hung it on his saddle.

"Thank you." She leaned back, resting on his chest. He held her around the waist as she snuggled next to his heart.

"You are the bravest woman I have ever met," he said. "I don't know if I could have spent two hours in that hellhole, let alone the twenty-eight hours you were there."

"So, it's been only a day?"

"It's been only a day," he said. Then he eyed the sky. "Well, now closer to two days." She closed her eyes and leaned into his strength. "You got any beef jerky in there?"

"I know you're hungry, but I want to get back to town as soon as possible. I don't want anyone getting lucky and stumbling across us before we hit civilization."

Suddenly Donovan's horse shied. Lillian grabbed hold of Donovan's waist and held on as the horse let out a high-pitched neigh and leaped up onto its back legs.

"Whoa, what is it, boy?" Donovan said. Lillian could feel the strain in his back and legs as he barely held them in place on the horse's back. Donovan's muscles bulged as he held her with one hand and used the rest of his body to control the horse beneath them.

Donovan was able to get the horse to slow down after a few hundred yards. All three were breathing hard when they came out onto a path that bordered the mountainside. Cold air whipped over Lillian's heated skin.

"Okay, now. It's okay," Donovan soothed. Lillian didn't know if he was talking to her or the horse. It didn't matter really. They all needed the calming. He walked the animal in small, tight circles until it calmed a bit more. Then he stopped and got down. He stroked the horse's big head and whispered in its ear. Lillian could feel its rapid heartbeat under her.

"I don't know what spooked him, but we all need a break." Donovan raised his arms and helped Lillian dismount.

"The horse looks bad. Have you been traveling nonstop since I was taken?"

"We need to find water," Donovan said, his tone grim. "And we need to try to keep cover."

"You think they'll find out I'm gone?"

"I think it's best to count on that." Donovan nodded. "Are you okay to walk?"

"I'm good."

Donovan walked down the trail. "Let's keep moving. It's best for the horse. We have to find water, and we have to find cover."

Lillian pushed her heavy legs forward. The path was rocky but free of debris. They followed it down the mountain, keeping one side always against the rocky face.

The horse neighed softly. Lillian could hear the small sound of water trickling. Donovan pointed. At the next curve in the road, he took them carefully off the track. A few feet below ran a slight stream. The steep bank held the edge of the path.

The horse went straight for the water. Donovan reached down

and scooped up a handful. He tasted it. "It's good, ice melt. Cold as hell, but clean."

Lillian joined them at the stream. She knelt down and cupped handfuls of the cool water, washed her face and hands, and drank her fill.

They weren't there but a few moments before they heard horses coming down the trail at a fast clip. Donovan put his finger to his lips and then handed her a pistol. Lillian took it. Concern filled her. Donovan motioned for her to head down the stream and then to hide under the brush.

She nodded and sent him a questioning look. He put his hands on his twin Colts and motioned for her not to worry.

Grabbing her hand, he placed it against his fast-beating heart. In the silence they embraced. His lips met hers and the kiss pierced her soul. Sad, sweet, and full of promise, the kiss spoke volumes even as he cut it short. Donovan raised his head. His beautiful blue eyes looked deep into hers. "Go," he said. "No matter what, stay alive."

The sound of galloping horses grew. Her heart raced as if to keep up with it. She lifted her skirts and sloshed through the water. When she was a hundred or so feet from Donovan, she climbed up the bank and crawled belly first under the branches of a scrub tree.

She peered out between the branches and realized that the sky was no longer deep black but had turned a pewter gray. The sun was coming up. She prayed the galloping horses were a rescue party and not more of the men who had pulled her from her home.

Donovan eased his horse up the side bank and left it to nibble on the young grasses that grew along the stream. Then he took up a position with his back against the trunk of a large aspen and tracked the sound of horses as they came down the mountain.

He knew it wasn't a rescue party. The only people up that mountain were the men who had Lillian in that cellar. If he were the cold-blooded kind, he'd take aim and pick them off one by one as they came around the mountain. In his mind, they deserved no less for what they'd done.

He hadn't had time to ask her if they'd touched her. But the bruises he saw on the side of her face in the dawning light told him all he needed to know.

Pressed against a tree trunk, he hoped they wouldn't see him, that the men would keep riding down the mountain.

That hope died when he heard them slow a few hundred yards up. They weren't in scope distance yet. The sound of galloping dissipated on the wind. The riders had gone to cover. He glanced up at the sky and noted the streaks of red shooting over the tops of the mountains. Daylight was coming and with it they would lose their cover.

He was miles from the path that led to Foster's mine, where the posse would be heading today. There was no way they would know to look on the trail where he and Lillian were. That meant it was him against whoever dared to hurt his woman.

He could live with that.

Donovan's ears perked up. Someone on horseback moved through the underbrush, following the creek bank on his side of the trail. Easing around the tree, he set the rifle on his shoulder and peered through the scope.

A man wearing a black felt hat and a buffalo plaid flannel shirt walked his horse through the underbrush. His gaze fixed on the ground. He was looking for something.

Donovan figured he was looking for the place they had gone off the trail. It was clearly marked. He hadn't taken the time to cover it. Trees rustled in the breeze above him. He watched the man draw closer.

With his finger on the trigger, he waited. It was a gamble. Donovan figured the man would shout once he discovered their trail, so he needed to take him out before then. But the sound of the rifle would bring the others running anyway. He bided his time.

The man was a few yards away when he caught site of their trail. He dismounted and squatted down to check the depth and direction of the track. Donovan made a quick decision.

Getting up, he took that moment, made a running leap across the stream, and landed on the man. A silent grapple ensued. Donovan beat the man with the butt of the rifle. The sound of his nose breaking was satisfying. The man groaned and pushed up, but Donovan held him with his knees to the man's biceps and hit him again with the butt of the rifle.

The man's eyes rolled back, and he fell to the ground. His horse made a neighing sound. Donovan's horse answered. The sound had his heart going strong. He rolled off the man and found a position along the edge of the bank. Two more men came around. One had his arm in a sling. The other was the biggest bruiser Donovan had even seen.

There was no way he was going to take that man out in hand-to-hand combat.

He eyed them through the scope. The man with the sling was Bart Johnson. Donovan snarled. So he was the person Lillian shot. Good for her. Donovan figured his best chance was to take out the big guy first and deal with Bart second.

Taking careful aim, Donovan slowly squeezed the trigger. Before he got the shot off he felt cold steel pressed behind his ear.

"I wouldn't do that if I were you, son." A man's raspy voice had a cold sweat popping out on Donovan's forehead. "Put the gun down and your hands up. Slowly."

Donovan did as the man commanded, raising his hands and getting up on his knees.

The man kicked the rifle away out of reach. Keeping the gun shoved against Donovan's head, he pulled the remaining pistol out of Donovan's gunbelt.

"Stand up," the man said. "I think you and I have a thing or two to say to each other."

Donovan stood, his hands in the air. The two men on horseback froze when they spotted Donovan coming up the bank.

"What'cha got there, Emit?" Bart asked. He leaned down to get a closer look. "Well, my, my, if it ain't the famous Donovan West." Bart sent him a feral grin. "If you're here, that means your witch ain't too far. Don't worry, we'll find her. Emit here's half Indian. He can track a bug on a rock. Can't you, Emit?"

"I reckon."

Donovan narrowed his eyes. Helpless, he prayed that Lillian would have the good sense to stay hidden, and if that didn't work, that she had the good aim to shoot whoever found her right between the eyes.

Chapter Seventeen

Lillian wanted to scream at Donovan to watch out. Instead, she watched helplessly as the second man snuck up on him. Donovan had told her to hide, to survive.

She was used to doing that. Used to caring for no one but herself. Her heart thudded heavy and swift against her chest. This time was different; she wasn't used to the panic that swamped her at seeing her man in danger. The pulse point in her belly pounded out her terror as she lay in the underbrush near the stream.

She was good. She could shoot the man with the gun to Donovan's head. But she wasn't sure that he wouldn't pull the trigger as her bullet hit him.

To make matters worse, two more men came down the trail. These two she recognized immediately. One was the giant of a man who had hauled her unceremoniously across his shoulders. The other was Bart Johnson. She should have aimed for that one's heart when she'd had the chance.

"Live and learn," she muttered. Her breath pushed dust up from the ground, she was so close. It tickled her nose, and she did all she could not to sneeze and give herself away.

The two men on horseback spoke to Donovan. He must not have given them the answers they wanted. The man with the gun slammed the butt of it into Donovan's jaw, dropping him to his knees.

Lillian bit the inside of her cheek. The smart thing to do would be to stay hidden. Save herself. Lillian had told Donovan she wasn't a team player. She had warned him she was selfish and no good.

He had risked his life to save her. Even though this was all his fault, she couldn't just lie here and watch them beat Donovan to a pulp.

Decision made, she drew the Colt up to her face to get a good angle. She figured the best thing to do was to take out the big man first. Hopefully she could do it with one shot. The man with Donovan would turn to see where the shot came from. If she were fast enough, she could take him out next.

That left Bart. It was a gamble. Bart could kill Donovan if he got a shot off fast enough. But Lillian knew that Bart would have to use his left hand, which should slow him down. She had put enough buckshot into his right hand to keep it from working for a while.

There could be other men coming down the trail. She bit her lip and watched Donovan stagger to his feet. Bart barked out something. Donovan didn't move. The third man raised his hand as if to beat Donovan again.

Lillian went for it. Heart pounding, she took a slow breath in and out as she squeezed the trigger. It all happened quickly, but Lillian saw it as if each moment were frozen in time. The bullet hit the big man between the eyes. He looked stunned. Then he fell over with a crashing thud.

Bart's horse reared. The third man swung his pistol around and shot in her general direction, giving her time to aim. She squeezed again, and her bullet went straight to his heart. He got another shot off in her direction before he crumbled.

She felt something whiz passed her, ricochet off the dirt, bounce up, and burn along her cheek. She tasted blood, but kept her hands steady, her aim on Bart's heart.

He fought to contain his horse and pull his gun left-handed. Donovan had ducked at the sound of the first shot and rolled toward the horses. Frightened by his action, Lillian wondered if he had gone mad. Surely he would be trampled. She watched as he stopped just under the horses' noses. At that angle, Bart could not shoot him.

"Draw," Lillian shouted to Bart. "I dare you."

He raised his hands instead, and she discovered she was disappointed. She had hoped he would give her an excuse to shoot him.

"Bitch," Bart said, his tone shocked. "You just killed two men in cold blood."

Lillian stood up. "I hoped to kill three."

"You won't kill me," he said and sneered. "You already had your chance and only wounded me."

"Go for your gun and see," Lillian dared him.

"I wouldn't." Donovan took the big man's horse by the reins and was careful to keep the animal between him and Bart. "I believe she will kill you."

Bart narrowed his eyes. "This is all your fault, West," he said. "If you had just left well enough alone, we would have never had to take her." He turned his beady eyes on Lillian. "He's the one you should shoot. He lied to you. I don't know what he told you he was doing, but it ain't true. He's been riding all over the territory with that buddy of his. Who knows? He may have women everywhere."

"That's between him and me," Lillian said, unconcerned with Bart's accusations. "Now, take out your gun, nice and slow."

She walked toward him, keeping her gun steady by holding it with both hands.

He pulled the gun out with his good hand and his fingers on the butt. She cocked her Colt. "Throw it on the ground in front of Donovan." He paused and looked from her to Donovan. "Do it!" she demanded and stopped at the edge of the stream. There was still plenty of distance between her and Bart, first the stream, then the bank, and then Donovan and the two horses. She kept the stream between them so that Bart would have to choose one or the other if he decided to be stupid and shoot.

The gun hit the dirt at Donovan's feet with a thud.

"Good. Now, get down."

Bart frowned. He grunted and groaned, but dismounted.

His shot-up hand and shoulder hindered him enough to make his progress slow.

Donovan bent down and picked up Bart's gun. Checking the chamber, he pointed it at the man.

"Now come around the front," Donovan said. Bart took a step. "With your hands in the air."

"Don't do anything you might regret," Lillian said as she kept her gun aimed at Bart.

"I shoulda done you last night," Bart sneered. "You'd be too wore out to shoot anyone this morning."

Donovan hauled off and plowed his fist into Bart's face. The man crumpled like a sack of feed. Donovan shook his fist to ward off the sting. Lillian couldn't help the smile. She uncocked her gun and slipped it into the waistband of her apron. Then she crossed the stream and climbed up onto the trail.

Donovan took rope from the big guy's saddle and hog-tied Bart. Then he unceremoniously tossed him up on the back of the horse.

Now that it was over, Lillian trembled. Her knees knocked just a bit. She clung to the big man's horse to keep her footing so that Donovan couldn't see how weak she really was. "I told you I don't die easy," she commented as she watched him pick the third man up under the arms and drag the body next to the body of the big man.

"I told you to stay hidden and survive." His tone was not a happy one. It was as if he scolded her for saving his life. That got her back up.

"Yeah, well, I did what I thought was best." She raised her chin in defiance. "If it weren't for me, you might be dragged halfway to Leadville by now."

"And you would be safe and sound." He straightened and put his hands on his hips. "You could have been shot." He narrowed his eyes at her. Then he cursed something dark under his breath and stormed toward her.

She couldn't help it. Lillian took two steps back, away from his anger. He reached out, and she stuck her chin out. Let him just try to hit her.

Instead, he put his hand under her chin and eyed her cheek. "You did get shot, you idiot woman," he said.

"I most certainly did not." She pulled away from his touch. "I would know if I got shot."

"There's a deep rut right along your cheek." He pulled a handkerchief out of his pants pocket and dabbed at her cheek. "You're going to have a scar."

"Give me that." She pulled the handkerchief away from him. "So what if I have a scar?" She pressed the cloth against her cheek. It stung like heck. She pulled it away and sure enough there was fresh blood on it. "It's not like you'll be stuck with an ugly wife."

She pushed past him, intent on washing her face in the stream. He grabbed her by the arms and spun her to face him.

"You are not ugly," he said. "Foolish, maybe, but you'll never be ugly." Then he pulled her to him and kissed her.

Finally, she thought. She wound her hands around his neck and leaned into the strength of him. He was warm and solid against her. His mouth was tender and fierce. He tasted of sweat and dirt and an emotion she couldn't name. Didn't want to name.

He lifted her by her bottom, and she wrapped her legs around his waist. She kissed his lips, his jaw, his neck, the pulse point at the edge of his collar bone. He muttered her name over and over, and she felt as if she would burst with emotion. Relief, safety, love, desire.

Donovan winced when her hands touched the welts on his face.

She looked at him for a long moment. "We're a mess."

"Yes."

"What are we going to do now?"

"We need to get back to town."

"Your horse." The animal waited patiently in the cool morning shade of the aspens. "I'll go bring him up here."

"Okay," Donovan said. "I'll get these bodies on this horse. We'll take them all to the sheriff and see what he wants to do about things."

Lillian gathered up his horse. When she reached the trail, he had both bodies tied to the back of the big man's horse. With Bart lying unconscious over his saddle, there was nothing for them to do but find their way down the mountain.

"How did you know where to find me?" she asked.

"It's a long story."

"We've got nothing but time," she said. "I believe we're still a couple hours out of town."

"All right," he said. "It all started with a note sending me to Foster's mine . . ."

Lillian listened to the tone of his voice. Deep and warm, it rumbled through her like the sound of a cello. She liked the way it made her blood hum in her veins and decided she could listen to him talk forever.

The idea scared her more than anything had ever scared her in her life.

Chapter Eighteen

Lillian primped before the mirror that hung over her dresser. For the first time in her life, she was going to a dance. Like Cinderella, she had a brand-new fancy gown, new slippers and hair ribbons. She also had a handsome prince whose arm she would walk in on.

It was all a dream she hadn't even known she wanted. She bit her lips to pinken them and then pinched her unmarked cheek to bring color to her face. She didn't wear face powder. She never had and, frankly, wasn't interested in it now. Still, it would have been nice to have something other than bruises, which were turning ugly yellow and black along her jaw. Something to hide the thick scab that ran about two inches along her cheek.

The best she could do was hide it with the tulle she had artfully draped across her hat so that the wounded side of her face was less visible. There was nothing left to do but put on the kid gloves she had bought for this occasion and go out and face the world.

The store had been swamped all day. People had come in to see how she was and to purchase goods for their Founders Day celebrations.

Donovan stood in the doorway. He leaned against the door jamb, his arms crossed over his chest. His gaze poured over her in a hard and possessive way. It made her heart flutter and her hands tremble.

"I'm ready." She moved toward him to hide the effect he had on her.

He straightened. "You look stunning."

"Thank you." She wasn't used to compliments, and Donovan had a way of tossing them out willy-nilly.

But after all they had been through, she trusted him. He had explained how the men they had taken down were only small pawns in a bigger scheme. How he and Mac were planning to root out the mastermind and rid the county of bad guys. The thought made her smile. She was certain that sometime tonight there would be a scene at the dance. That Mr. Sandler would be arrested and the entire scheme would be uncovered.

She took a deep breath and blew it out slowly. Then Donovan would be done with his assignment and he and Kane would go back to Washington, D.C., where they'd come from.

The thought of it made her heart squeeze and the back of her eyes sting. She brushed it away. She would cross that bridge when she came to it. After all, she had done just fine without Donovan. It would be just fine again.

"You can hear the music all the way down the street." Donovan opened the door and led her out onto the boardwalk that connected all the false fronts.

He was right. The sound of a band playing drifted up from the square, along with the sounds of people talking and laughing. The streets were crowded with couples dressed to the nines.

Donovan wore a pair of fine wool pants in black, a white dress shirt with a thin red tie, and a lovely paisley gray waistcoat. Topping it all off was a suit coat that appeared to be cut for him. Perhaps Mrs. Quidly, the town seamstress, had made the coat just for him.

She blinked in surprise at the jealousy that thought brought her. Mrs. Quidly was quite pretty. But Donovan had his hand on Lillian's back. It was Lillian he guided toward the crowd.

She knew it was all for show. He might like her pie, but he was not promised to her. The only reason he was with her now was to keep up the pretense they were married for his mission.

"Mr. and Mrs. West," Mr. Huckabee called behind them.

Donovan stopped and shook hands. Lillian gave Mrs. Huckabee a hug and a kiss. The older woman had been wonderful ever since she had come back. Lillian wondered how long the guilt would last. She hid a smile at the thought.

"I'm so glad you are feeling better." Mrs. Huckabee took Lillian's arm. The women walked in front of the men. Lillian could hear Mr. Huckabee asking Donovan what he thought about extraditing Bart to Denver for the federal courts.

"I'm fine, really." Lillian patted Mrs. Huckabee's hand. The town square was a thick block of grass and paths that anchored the center of the town. On one side was the courthouse with its tall clock tower. On another was the church. The third street was Main Street, which was full of false-fronted stores. Then there was Pine Street, where the mayor had his mansion and was building a fancy hotel.

The square was decorated with red, white, and blue bunting that traveled from lampposts to the gazebo in the center. Inside the white gazebo the band played. Outside, couples strolled. Children ran around dressed in their finest. Three boys played kick the can. Another rolled a hoop.

"Oh, there's Alice. I must speak to her. I'll talk to you later, dear." Mrs. Huckabee scooted off to gossip with her best friend.

Lillian enjoyed the playful crowd. Donovan put his hand on her elbow and escorted her through the families and couples. Finally he found a nice spot under a tree.

"Wait here," he said. "I'll go grab us a bench." Lillian watched him dodge the crowd and call out to the other men as he picked up a wooden bench from a small stack and brought it over. She thought he was the best-looking man there. It seemed so natural for him to be there with her . . . getting a bench. It was as if they were a real couple, a part of the community that had been there forever, would be there forever.

What a strange idea.

"They have lemonade." Donovan put the bench down under the tree. "Have a seat, I'll bring you some."

"I'm capable of getting my own."

"I know." His blue gaze locked with hers. "For tonight, let me do this small thing."

She heard regret in his voice and wondered if he thought her kidnapping was somehow his fault. Lillian had tried reassuring him, letting him off the hook, but he refused to do anything other than wait on her hand and foot. "All right."

"Good, I'll bring you a plate as well."

They feasted on ham and beans and various salads. Someone had made brisket. An abundance of homemade rolls and desserts filled tabletops, making them groan. Lillian enjoyed it all.

At dusk, lanterns were strung up along the bunting to light the grounds. Donovan lay with his head in Lillian's lap. She stroked his fine hair, memorizing his sharp features with her fingers.

He grabbed her hand and turned it, placing a kiss on her exposed wrist. His lips were warm against her pulse, and she felt her heart flutter. Donovan opened his eyes, and she knew he understood how much he could move her.

"I haven't seen Mr. Sandler," she said, in an attempt to defuse the tension that sparked between them.

"He's here," Donovan said. "Don't worry. Everything is in place."

She smiled down at him. "You look so relaxed. No one would suspect you have any idea what is going on."

"Thank you." He stood and held out his hand. "Dance with me?"

"I'm not a very good dancer." The flush of embarrassment climbed up her face. He must have caught her watching the dancers with longing.

"It's all right," Donovan said. "Trust me. I won't lead you astray."

She put her hand in his. "I'm afraid you already have."

Escorting her to the area set out for dancing, he drew her into the whirling crowd. He put her hand on his shoulder and held the other in his, and she had no choice but to follow. It was a happy country dance, and she felt as if she were skipping and then flying. He guided her expertly and soon she moved with the ease of the other dancers.

She looked up into his smiling eyes and smiled back. The

dark sky above them twinkled with stars. The colors of the dresses and the exhilaration of being alive filled her senses. The music slowed to a waltz, and she found that somehow, when Donovan led, she could follow. They drew close and dipped and swirled, bodies brushing, fingers entwined.

This moment could go on forever. She opened her mouth to tell him just that when the sound of gunfire ricocheted through the crowd. Donovan had her shoved behind him in an instant.

Women screamed. Children ran. Men reached for guns that were not there. After all, this was supposed to be a celebration.

Six men on horseback galloped through the square, shooting into the air. They halted their animals near the band so hard that the horses jumped onto back legs, their hooves flailing in the faces of partygoers.

"What is the meaning of this?" demanded the mayor from the gazebo. The band stopped playing, and a strange silence filled the air.

The six men searched the crowd. Their gazes were mean and snake-eyed. "This here's a raid." The lead man pointed his gun at the men who had formed a line in front of the women. "Someone in this town's been selling us phony money and we wants revenge."

"Wait. They caught the counterfeit ring," the mayor explained. "We have the main culprit jailed right now."

"That don't give us our hard-earned silver back." The man spit.

"We can't replace what they stole, but we can see they get justice." The mayor's hands were up.

"Justice ain't gonna feed our bellies come winter," the oily man said. "Right, boys?"

The other men hollered and shot their guns in the air. From the corner of her eye, Lillian saw Mrs. Huckabee faint. Two women went to her rescue, but the big man in front pointed his gun at them. "Leave her."

The women stopped, frozen in their tracks.

"We want the women on one side and the men on the other."

"Now see here," the mayor said.

"No, you see," the big man said and shot the mayor. The crowd gasped as the rotund man fell backward. Lillian felt Donovan's hand on her arm.

"Get down," he whispered.

"This wasn't part of your plan, was it?"

Donovan glanced at her. "Neither were you."

"I said I want the women on one side and men on the other." The ugly man raised his guns, pointing at Mr. Huckabee.

The men reluctantly stepped to the side. Lillian could feel the fear in the crowd. She gathered up Rebecca and the other younger women and tucked them in behind her. Only she knew of the small derringer she had strapped to her knee. After her last adventure she had vowed not to ever leave the house unarmed again. Besides the gun, she had a small knife sheathed in her waistband where she could get her hands on it quick if there was a need.

"Good," the lead man said.

The mayor moaned and sat up clutching his shoulder. Blood bloomed around his hand.

"Well, lookie there, I didn't kill him after all." The fat man's gaze weaved over the women. "Maybe I'll be lenient." He grinned. "Maybe not." He leaned on his saddle. "You sure got yourselves some fine-looking ladies. Better hope your men come up with enough money to cover our losses or we just might have to take it out in flesh."

The women gasped. Lillian hugged the girls and whispered for them not to listen.

The men strained toward the riders, but several strategically placed gunshots held the crowd at bay.

"Listen up, gentlemen," the gangster called out. "My men are going to pass around their hats. You fill them with everything you got on you, and we mean everything. If you come up with enough to cover our expenses, then we'll ride out of here and never look back." He leaned down and spit. "You skimp and think you can keep something from us, and I'll pick out a couple of these fillies and have my way with them right now."

Another woman fainted dead away. The man laughed, showing rotting teeth. "Pass the hats, boys. I'm ready to have me some fun."

Two of the miners broke ranks and held out their hats while the men in town emptied their pockets.

"Pocket watches, money clips, guns, knives, even them fancy tie tacks," the big man ordered. "Hold nothing back."

"This is an outrage," said Mr. Huckabee as he reluctantly placed a chained pocket watch in the hat. "We aren't the ones who scammed you."

"Don't matter to me if you were or not," the big guy said. "What matters is that I get what's coming to me. You can have fun getting those what scammed us and stringing them up. I ain't got time for that."

The two men made their rounds and then returned to the man in charge. They looked over their booty.

"Now, this is right sad." The big man held up a fist full of goods. "Pitiful. Jethro, I want you to collect everything the ladies have."

The women gasped. Several grabbed the necklaces around their throats.

"Everything?" Jethro waggled dirt-blackened brows.

"Just their goods, for now." The leader man grinned. "We'll see after that."

"Now see here." Mr. Huckabee took a step forward. The big man cocked his gun and pointed it at the barber. He shut his mouth and stepped back.

Another lady fainted.

Lillian stepped forward. "Let me collect it. All your men will do is scare these poor women to death, and it's going to take much longer for you to get your payment if they are lying on the ground."

The big man looked her up and down. "Fine, but if it ain't enough, I get to take you too."

The girls behind Lillian wept loudly. "Fine."

"Then it's a deal. Jethro, give her your hat."

"Aw, you take away all my fun," Jethro said, his horse restless under him. "I was looking forward to searching the ones on the ground myself."

Lillian grabbed his filthy hat out of his hands. "Maybe next time," she said low enough for him to hear.

He leaned down and flashed a toothless grin. "Maybe the boss will let me search you when he's done."

"Touch me and die!" She stormed back toward the women. She helped them remove their earbobs and necklaces and rings. She was the first to put her wedding ring in the hat and all the others followed.

Mrs. Bitterman sobbed. "It is the only jewelry I have."

Lillian patted her arm. "It's just gold. We can replace gold."

"Hurry up there, girl," the big man called. "This is taking far too much time."

Lillian ground her teeth and quickly took the earbobs and necklaces off the ladies who were out cold and then gave the hat to the leader. "This should more than cover your needs."

"My needs are changing every minute." He looked at her as if she were naked. Lillian lifted her chin. Let him look. She'd kill him before he could touch her.

"Feisty." He chuckled and looked down into the hat and did some fast calculating. "Well, boys, looks like these are pretty generous folks, all told." He pursed his fat lips. "Still, we're going to need some protection on our way out of here." He pointed his gun at Lillian. "Come on, girly, you are going to see that no one shoots at us on the way out."

"No one will shoot," she said. "Go. You got what you wanted."

"I want you."

"You can't have her." Donovan shoved his way to the front of the crowd. He had a six-shooter in his hand. "Touch her, and I'll kill you."

The entire pack of wild men clicked their guns and pointed them at Donovan. Lillian's heart raced. Stupid man was going to get himself killed.

"Now, don't be an idiot, son," the big man said. "I won't take her far."

"You won't take her at all." Donovan's face was set like steel. Lillian knew he had six bullets. There were five men. What were the odds that Donovan could kill them all and not get killed? Not very good.

Not to mention all the men behind Donovan who could get hit by flying bullets.

"It's all right, Donovan," she said. "Let me go."

"Yeah, let her go, Donovan," Jethro mocked.

"No," the stubborn man said.

Lillian sighed. Donovan didn't leave her with many choices. She had no idea what the original plan was, if help was on the way or not. All she knew was that she had one shot if she pulled her derringer. That shot would only be good for distraction and a lot of innocent people could get hurt.

"Let me go," she said slowly. "Too many people here will get hurt if you shoot."

"Do ya hear that, boy? Put down your gun and let her go."

"No."

Tension was thick as a pea soup fog. A trickle of sweat itched the back of Lillian's neck. She looked at the women. "Get down, all of you!"

The women gasped and fell to the ground. The miners looked from Donovan to the group of ladies now prone on the ground. It was a brief instant but long enough to pull the men's attention away from Donovan and the others.

Art Miller jumped out and grabbed the reins of the man nearest him. He grabbed his gun and socked him. Donovan shot Jethro in the right hand, sending the gun flying toward Lillian.

Lillian grabbed it as the men mobbed the miners. Shots rang out. Lillian didn't know who was shooting. The sound of fist hitting flesh and horses screaming filled her ears as she raised the purloined gun and aimed it straight at the leader of the gang.

He turned as if to shoot her. She squeezed the trigger, hitting him square, knocking him to the ground. The smell of gun smoke and blood filled the air. The men mobbed the miners. Women screamed. Someone grabbed her from behind. She fought, only to hear Kane McCormick's voice in her ear.

"It's okay. It's me. We got this covered. Give me the gun."

Lillian looked into Kane's beautiful face and stopped struggling. She handed him the gun. It was then she noticed the other men who swarmed into town. They had what appeared to be five men tied up running behind a wagon. The wagon had a tarp over it, but Lillian knew it was the gold supply.

Everything was chaos. "Donovan?"

"I haven't seen him yet," Kane said.

"Wait, Mr. Sandler—"

"The sheriff got him before the miners came in."

"So you saw all that?"

"We were waiting for them to ride out," Kane said. "Fewer people to get hurt."

"Donovan—"

"Knew we had them surrounded." Kane squeezed her arms. "He didn't put his life in jeopardy recklessly."

"When I see him, I'm going to—"

"Lillian, come quick," Mr. Huckabee called through the mad chaos.

The sound of urgency in his voice had Lillian's heart leaping into her throat. She picked up her skirts and made a mad dash toward the barber. He took her by the arm and wove her through the milling crush.

"It's Donovan. He's been shot."

Chapter Nineteen

For the first time that night, fear snaked down Lillian's back. "Is Donovan all right?"

"You'd better come. Bob Cummins took him over to Doc's place."

A crowd of men milled about outside the doctor's house. She heard the mayor yelling something colorful inside.

"Make way!" Mr. Huckabee and Mac saw to it that Lillian got inside the small building. She passed a room where the mayor sat gulping whiskey while Doc's wife patched up his wounded shoulder.

The two men pulled her into the back room. It was a room that usually held the dead. A ghost trickled along the back of her neck when she entered the dark room. It was a feeling the nuns at the orphanage had said meant someone walked on your grave.

Only one lamp shone in the corner. Donovan lay on the bed. His skin was as white as the sheets, his lips a funny blue.

Lillian's heart cramped, stealing her breath. She stumbled toward him. "Donovan?" she whispered his name. When she touched him, he was cold, as if he were already leaving her. "Darn it, Donovan, what did you do?"

"He got himself good and shot," Mr. Huckabee said. "Don't know for sure what happened. One minute he was shooting the bugger on the horse, the next he was at my feet. Still as a rag doll."

Lillian took Donovan's hand in hers. She pressed it, limp

and cool, to her chest. Tears stung the back of her eyes. "Donovan."

He rolled his head toward her but did not open his eyes. She saw the stress of pain in the brackets around his mouth. The ashen look around his eyes. She kissed him. "Don't you die on me! We have too much to discuss for you to die on me."

"Clear the room." Doc washed his hands and dried them on a towel. "That means everyone. Including you, Lillian."

"I'm not going anywhere."

"You are," Doc said firmly. "I can't work on a man with you hovering. Mr. Huckabee, Mr. McCormick, take her home. Get her some tea and a warm blanket. She looks a bit shocky."

"I will not go." Lillian dug in her heels. "I won't leave him."

"You have to. You ain't got a choice." Doc nodded and Kane picked Lillian up and threw her over his shoulder before she could think to fight.

"Donovan!" she screamed as he carried her out the back of the building and into the cold night air.

A month went by in a blur. Lillian wore her widow's weeds like a badge. She had been loved. All her other accomplishments fell away in comparison. The rest was simply survival.

The town had a new respect for her. She didn't feel as if she had earned it, but there was nothing she could say to dissuade them. Living in a mining town was rough business. People died young. Many died in horrible ways. At least Donovan had gone quickly.

Thanks to Donovan, Lillian no longer had to pretend. She was able to sign for her own goods and pay her own bills. It was little consolation.

The bells on the store doors jangled and Lillian looked up from her account books to see Kane McCormick coming across the room. He halted at the counter and leaned against it, studying her.

"Kane!" She came around and hugged him. He took the embrace warmly and then set her on her feet an arm's length away.

"How are you, Lillian?"

"I'm okay."

"No, really," he said. "How are you?"

She let her gaze go from his lovely face to the dress shirt he wore under his suit coat. "I miss him."

"Are you happy?"

"What a strange question."

He took her by the arm and gently led her to one of the two chairs that sat by the potbelly stove. "Lillian." He sat down across from her and leaned in, taking her hands in his. "There is something I have to know. Something I've come to ask."

"What?"

"Lillian," he said and squirmed a bit.

She squeezed his hands. "What?"

"We're friends, right?"

She smiled at him. "Of course."

"You would tell me if you were in trouble, right?"

"What do you mean?"

He looked deep into her eyes. She blinked at him and then suddenly it dawned on her. She gave him a sad smile. "Oh, no. We never . . . I'm not in the family way, if that's what you want to know." She squeezed his hands and let go. It was strange to be discussing such a thing with a man, especially since he wasn't Donovan. "I wish we had," she said, her tone soft so as not to carry. Not that it mattered. The store was quiet right now. "I wish I had some part of Donovan with me."

"You were in love with him."

"Am in love with him," she corrected him. "For all his arrogance and bossiness, I still love him. I've never had that before . . ."

"Had what?"

"Someone who cared about me. Someone to step in front of me in times of danger." She looked at him. "I was left at an orphanage when I was three."

"You didn't have any family?"

"No, I didn't know what I was missing until Donovan." She paused. "Kane, what was his real name? Can you tell me?"

"His real name should be Idiot," Kane muttered. Lillian

couldn't tell what he meant by that, but she figured they had been friends for years. Kane must miss him as much as she missed him. "Listen, Lillian, I have a favor to ask of you."

She drew her eyebrows together in confusion. "Okay . . ."

"I know that running the store by yourself is a big job." He put up his hand to stop her when she went to speak. "Hear me out. I have a friend. He's a good man, if not a bit of an idiot. He got himself shot up and will probably walk with a cane the rest of his life."

"Kane?"

"He used to be a lawman, but since he got hurt he can't ride like he used to. So, I thought, what with you being a widow and all, you could use an extra hand."

"Well . . ."

"Why don't you meet him before you make up your mind. He's right outside." Kane left before she could answer.

Lillian stood and wrung her hands. She really didn't need a hired hand. Between Bruce and her shotgun she had the place covered. Still, everyone knew she was a widow now. It would help to have a man around to keep people from thinking she could be pushed around.

The doorbells jangled and Kane walked in. Behind him was a man leaning heavily on a cane as he walked. He wore a soft blue shirt and dark trousers. He had a hat covering most of his face as he watched the floor for trip spots.

"Lillian West, I would like to introduce you to Patrick Scott Donovan."

The man lifted his head and looked her in the eye.

"Donovan?" Lillian's heart stopped and her mouth went dry.

"Patrick Scott Donovan, at your service, ma'am." She knew that voice. She knew that face. With an uncontrollable squeal she threw herself at him. He stumbled back, and they both ended up on the floor.

Lillian kissed him right then and there with no hesitation. The best part was he kissed her back.

"Well, I'll be." Kane took off his hat and wiped his forehead. "She didn't shoot us both."

Lillian put her hands on the floor on either side of Donovan's face. He looked good. His color was still pale, but there was happiness in his dark eyes. "I should shoot you both." She frowned at him. "Come to think of it, I do keep a derringer in my pocket."

She reached down and Donovan grabbed her hand and sat up, hauling her into his lap. "Don't shoot. At least not Mac. This whole thing was my idea, not his."

She glanced at Kane and he shrugged. She frowned, her excitement dimming. "You wanted me to believe you were dead?" She got to her feet and put some distance between her and the man she loved.

"I wanted Donovan West dead." Donovan slowly got up. The effort had the skin around his mouth turning white. She rushed to get him a chair, and he sat. "I wanted that man out of the way, so that I could court you, Miss Lillian. So that I could do everything proper. And maybe, in time, you'll forgive me. And then maybe even say yes when I ask you to marry me."

She opened her mouth to speak but he raised his hand to stop her.

"I know how you feel about marriage."

"And I know you made a vow," she stated. "Well, I'm here to tell you I won't marry a man who won't give me children. I'm a sturdy thing, Donovan."

"Please call me Patrick."

"I don't die easy." She had her hands on her hips.

He smiled. It was a smile that warmed her heart and melted any anger she might have had. "I know." He nodded. "It's one of the things I love best about you. And someone told me that vows made in the heat of the moment can be broken once the head clears. That is, if a person can get around their own stubbornness."

"Oh." She stepped toward him involuntarily.

Kane coughed. "Well, my work here is done." He shoved his hat on his head. "I've got a case in Phoenix and a new partner on the train there."

Lillian hugged Kane and kissed him on his cheek. "Thank you. You'll come back for the wedding, won't you?"

"I don't know." Kane pursed his mouth. "These cases can take a few weeks." His eyes twinkled. "Are you going to wait that long to marry?"

Donovan took her hand and tugged her down onto his lap. "Not if I have anything to say about it."

"Well, then a kiss for the bride." Kane bent down and kissed her full on the mouth. "Congratulations! You know, Miss Lillian, you deserve better than this one. You change your mind, and I'm only a telegram away."

Warmth blossomed in Lillian's chest. She leaned back against Donovan, happier than she had ever been in her entire life. "I'll keep that in mind."

Kane chuckled and walked out. The doorbells jangled behind him, but Lillian barely heard them as Donovan kissed the life back into her.

They were married two weeks later. There was the usual gossip about two people getting hitched so quickly. A rumor floated around that it was because Patrick Scott Donovan looked like her first husband, only much thinner. Maybe his face was sharper, his cheekbones higher, and he walked with a bad limp. But if they didn't know better, they'd think Patrick Donovan was Donovan West. But then, people believed what they wanted to believe. They'd been through this before. Why, just when rumors had started flying that Lillian might not be married, her husband had shown up. No one wanted to be that wrong twice.

Besides, Donovan West had died; the entire town had turned out for the funeral. Doc had pronounced him dead and Doc would have no reason to lie. So speculation would stay just that: speculation. Everyone liked Lillian and was happy to see her so happy. No one wanted to go digging up a dead man only to see if a rumor was true. By the time Lillian's first son came along, no one could remember what Donovan West looked like, and the rumor died. Still, once a year someone put flowers on Donovan West's grave in memory of a man who helped save a town, and the lovely young woman who was one of their own.